The Lark
Shall Sing

Elizabeth Cadell

The Friendly Air Publishing

thefriendlyairpublishing.com

This book is a work of fiction. Names, locals, business, organizations, and incidents are products of the author's imagination or are used fictitiously. Any resemblance to actual events, locals, or persons, living or dead, is entirely coincidental.

"The lark shall sing me hame in my ain countree."

Allan Cunningham.

Chapter One

"It's a good photograph," said Mr. Milward, peering at it.

"Yes." His son, Jeff, adjusted his glasses and looked over his father's shoulder. "I took it from just in front of the big tree. The..."

"In the middle of the old lawn." Mr. Milward sighed. "It's a beautiful old house."

Jeff was not disposed to discuss the point. He had spent the morning there and anyone watching him would have seen only a serious young house-agent taking photographs of a property—but Jeff knew that he had gone out there less as a photographer than as a pilgrim; he had wandered round the garden and then he had gone into the house and he had sought out the places he knew best; the deep settee on the first landing; the study; the big window seat in the drawing room where he and Roselle had...

He pulled himself up sharply. It was over and done with, and if he were quite honest with himself, he would admit that the last three or four months hadn't been as bad as the first eight or nine. The wound was still smarting, he thought, prodding it exploringly; it was still there; it hadn't healed, but the gap, as it were, was closing. He could think of Roselle, now, without experiencing stabbing pains that seemed to go through his body and leave him feeling dull and shaken.

"You'd better look at the advertisement," he told his father.

"Ah!" Mr. Milward came to himself with a start; he, too, had been dreaming. He had allowed his mind to wander from his neat little office and dwell on Lucille; now he brought it back firmly and cleared his throat. "June, a good time to sell," he observed, taking the advertisement and glancing through it rapidly. "Now, let me see: For Sale, er um, er um." He paused with a frown. "*Two* bathrooms?"

"Don't you remember? Those people made that small attic room into a second one."

"So they did." Mr. Milward shifted a little in his chair, and looked up at his son. "They were splendid tenants."

"Yes," Jeff agreed, "they did a lot to the place. I thought when I was out there yesterday that it looked a good deal better now than it did a year ago, when—"

He stopped. The wound was almost healed; it would be unwise to reopen it.

"Yes, a year," mused Mr. Milward. "It's gone very quickly. Or perhaps—" He glanced at Jeff with something of questioning, something of sympathy in his glance— "perhaps you don't think so?"

"If you mean do I still miss Roselle—then yes, I do." admitted Jeff, a little unwillingly. "I was wondering yesterday—"

"Whether they'll come back?"

"Yes."

Mr. Milward leaned back, folded his hands, and gave the matter some thought. He was thin and grey-haired and bespectacled and a little shabby, with kind, wise old eyes. Jeff watched him, and waited.

"No," said Mr. Milward at last, "I don't think they'll come back."

"You mean you don't think Lucille will consider it?"

"If she's getting married to this fellow down in Cornwall—her letter was very definite. I showed it to your mother last night, and she agreed with me when I said that it sounded quite settled. Lucille will marry, and I don't see how the others could keep the house on without her— even if they wanted to. And they don't seem to want to. They—"

He paused. Jeff had walked to the window and was staring out, his back to his father, looking at the busy little High Street, and something in his attitude brought Mr. Milward's summary to a somewhat wavering end. It was a sad business, he reflected, taking up his pipe and filling it absently. It was distressing to see a splendid family like that breaking up. Perhaps he couldn't be called a family man—since Jeff was his only child—but he had family feeling. Yes, he had a good deal of family feeling, he thought soberly, and even if he hadn't, he

9

couldn't look on unmoved at this breaking up of a home that he had known for—how many?—thirty years at least. And even if he didn't like seeing the family separated, dispersed, spread about, he would regret saying good-bye to Lucille—perhaps because he had known her from her babyhood, perhaps because she was immeasurably his favourite godchild, perhaps because he had been a little in love with her mother—perhaps even because Lucille herself was so young and so lovely and so vital; chiefly, perhaps, because the past year had been a little bleak without her.

But things moved; things happened, and one had to accustom oneself and adapt oneself...If only Jeff had not been so deeply involved; he had thought lately that he had begun to put Roselle out of his mind, but it was now plain to see that he had been living through the past year hoping that they would all come back to live in the house....

The Waynes had gone away for a year. The year was now over—but they were not coming back. Lucille had written to say so; she would be here this morning, here in Greenhurst, here in this office to talk over the sale of the house—and, though it seemed incredible, when the visit was over, she would go back to Cornwall—to live among people he had never seen and might never see.

Lucille—and the others. After all these years. He had seen them almost as soon as they had come into the world: Lucille, his godchild; Nicholas, his wife's godson; Roselle... Simon...Julia...and then, last of all, Dominic. A fine family, people had always said—healthy, good-looking—all except Julia, that is—and all full of life and spirit and...Well, no; not all of them. Roselle was a gentle little thing and so was Simon. But the others had spirit enough and to spare. Lucille, perhaps, had too much. He had always warned her about her habit of acting too impetuously, too hastily, but who had ever been able to prevent Lucille from doing anything she wanted to do?

Lucille—lovely, lovely Lucille. His spirits rose a little. Even if she was coming only to complete this gloomy business, she would, at any rate, be with them for a few days; they would see her, and the sight of her would give immense pleasure to himself and to his wife. To Jeff? Perhaps not. Jeff judged Lucille, Mr. Milward thought, a little too harshly. He blamed her for the break-up of the family; he felt that she had sent Roselle away, out of his life. It was not strictly true, but perhaps if Lucille had been a little more patient...

He studied his son's sturdy shoulders against the window. A fine young man, Jeff. Not outstandingly handsome perhaps, but quiet and sturdy and reliable. Perhaps he might have done something better—perhaps they should have sent him away out of Greenhurst, away to something more than this partnership in the house-agent's business. But he had elected to stay here and live at home and work in his little office in the High Street—and after all, Mr. Milward reflected, it was a snug little business; the only one of its kind in Greenhurst; prospering and likely to go on prospering. It would have been no bad thing for Roselle to marry into— but she had had her chance and she had rejected it—rejected Jeff and Greenhurst and gone off to London. If Lucille had tried to argue with her, or persuade her—but she hadn't and there it was. It was really a circle, and it always came back in the end to the same thing: If Lucille had waited...

"Well," Jeff's voice roused him, "do you think the wording's all right?"

"Oh, let me see—yes, it seems so, on the whole. But I don't much care for Desirable Residence. Wouldn't Family House be better?"

"No, I don't think so. Family House nearly always means a ramshackle old barn of a place with endless bedrooms and no amenities. Besides, I'm putting it in *The Times* and *The Telegraph* and we might draw in some big fish who'll look down their noses at family houses. I rather want to add Sacrificial Price."

"I think Highly Recommended would do. Have it typed out, will you, and I'll show it to Lucille when she arrives."

"She's coming here first, isn't she? I mean, before going out to the house."

"Yes. Don't be late for the train, Jeff; the eleven two's always in on time. And try to persuade her not to stay out there all alone; she can stay with us and you can drive her over to Wood Mount whenever she wants to go."

Jeff went out, and Mr. Milward was left to go on with his work, but his mind was not on what he was doing. He looked at papers, signed letters and answered the telephone in his usual quiet, somewhat absent-minded way, but a series of pictures was passing through his mind, and some of them were so vivid that he found it difficult to remind himself of the number of years that had gone by since the scenes had been enacted. Lucille in tattered shorts, roaming round the beautiful, half-wild garden of Wood Mount, leading Nicholas—four years her junior—into mischief, even into danger. Roselle, a year younger than Nicholas, had seldom joined in the more riotous expeditions; she had usually, he remembered, remained on the touch line; she had trembled when they took risks, wept when the risks didn't come off, and fetched bandages in all the gory sequels.

That, perhaps, had been the happiest time, when their parents had been still young enough, still well enough to enjoy the children. Simon and Julia and Dominic had come too late, and their memories of their parents must be almost all sober ones: an ageing father, a frail and often peevish mother. Yes, there had been trouble enough then, and most of it had fallen on Lucille; those last few years had been hard for her. She had been—how old?—sixteen, when her father died, and from that time onwards, she had shouldered most of the responsibility of the household. Much as he had loved her mother, Mr. Milward could not help admitting that in the last years of her life she had been a very difficult and a very extravagant woman. Lucille had been housekeeper, nurse, mother to the younger ones; she had tried to impose economies, but it had been impossible to make her mother understand that money values had changed—and so the bills continued to come in and the money continued to pour out, until her mother's death two years ago.

Two years. Lucille had been twenty-two. Yes, Mr. Milward remembered, it must be two years ago almost to the day—and for the year after that, Lucille had kept on the house and tried to make ends meet. Then they had all gone—Nicholas, indeed, had already gone away to do his National Service—and now it was the turn of the others. Lucille had gone as secretary-companion to an old lady in Cornwall, Roselle had gone to work in London; Julia had gone as a boarder to school, Simon and Dominic had gone to live with a childless uncle and aunt in Shropshire. The house had been let, furnished, for a year. A year, Lucille had said, and now the year was up, the tenants had gone, but Lucille and her brothers and sisters were not coming back. Lucille had given up her post in Cornwall and was to be married—and the house was to be sold.

Mr. Milward sighed heavily. He had seen their parents married; he himself had sold them the house; he had watched the family grow—and now he was to see it disperse. He would lose his favourite, Lucille; his wife would lose Nicholas—and Jeff...well, Jeff was only twenty-four; young men of twenty-four...did they love for ever? Mr. Milward couldn't decide—but he knew that his son was not impulsive and not given to idle fancies. He had fallen in love with Roselle when she was sixteen—gentle little Roselle, who looked like a flower; she had loved him a little, but she had loved the thought of change even more...

, He was so deeply immersed in his memories that when he looked up and saw Lucille standing in the doorway, he had to pause for a moment before stumbling to his feet—pause to wonder whether he were still dreaming...But she was there—and she was as beautiful as she had been in his dreams, and his imagination had touched up the picture not a whit too much.

"Uncle Bill." She was beside him and she was pressing him back gently into his chair. Her arms were round him; she smelt of lilac and her lips—her lovely, soft, warm lips, were on his forehead, and then she was kissing him gently here and there—on his cheeks, his eyes, the tip of his nose, giving him a delicious feeling that he tried to describe, afterwards, to his wife and which she told him was not in the least god-fatherly.

"Ah—Lucille," was all he could say, and he knew it sounded dry and matter-of-fact and far from welcoming. But she had only given him seventeen kisses, and she always, when they had been apart for some time, liked to give him one for each year of her age. Eighteen...nineteen— nobody who saw her like this could ever again say that she had a streak of hardness in her nature. This was the real Lucille, and the other—the one people called hard or cold or overbearing—that was the Lucille who had learned, a little too early, that life could cease to be a matter of romping and become a harsh affair; that age and illness could turn indulgent parents into selfish or even neurotic patients. This...this was his own beloved Lucille. She

15

drew away from him and sat on the edge of his desk to study him frankly.

"Older; much, much older," she pronounced. "Uncle Bill, my pet, you've gone off terribly; you've got two more white hairs and your moustache has faded."

"Did Jeff meet you?"

"Yes. I came straight here—then I'm going to Wood Mount—and then I'll come back and see Aunt Maggie." She wasn't her aunt, just as he wasn't her uncle; his name wasn't Bill and his wife's wasn't Maggie, but Lucille had re-christened them both more than twenty years ago.

"She's got your bed ready; she says it's quite ridiculous to go out to the house and stay there all alone."

"But I'm going, darling—I must. Not to moon about there but to work—there are a thousand and one things to do, and I'd better be on the spot. What does the house look like?"

"It looks splendid. Jeff was out there this morning. I suppose he told you that. You've been very lucky; they were extremely good tenants. They put a bathroom in and they did up the downstairs rooms and they employed two gardeners—the garden certainly needed attention."

"Why didn't they want to stay on?"

"They couldn't. They had to go back to South Africa to see about some business there. But for that, I think they would have made an offer for the house—once I'd heard from you that you wanted to sell." He hesitated. "Lucille..."

"No, darling," she said instantly, "Jeff tried that, and it's no use. The house has got to go."

"A family is a family, Lucille."

"I know that, but we tried it for a year, didn't we? It isn't as though the moment Mother died, we scattered. We didn't; we tried it for a whole year—and you know perfectly well that we couldn't afford to stay on."

"But the others—"

"The others are perfectly happy. Roselle likes her job and she likes her flat; Julia's made no complaints, which means she hasn't got any; the boys are perfectly happy with Aunt Mary. After all, she begged and begged for them—you can't accuse me of posting them off like a couple of parcels. She wanted them—and they wanted to go."

"Little boys of that age don't know what they want, Lucille. And your Aunt Mary had no children of her own at that time, and—as far as I understand it—no prospect of any. Now she has a baby of her own, so—"

"—so she could have written to say that circumstances had changed, and so on and so *on*. But she didn't, darling."

"Perhaps she thought it would come better from you."

"Well," she smiled at him indulgently, "I'll write and ask her. If she doesn't want to keep them, they can come to me in Cornwall. In any case, they would spend as much time as possible with me."

"With..." Mr. Milward fidgeted nervously, "With you and

your husband?"

"Yes. His house is much larger than ours, and he's quite prepared to entertain all my family for indefinite periods— that was part of the bargain. Does that make you feel better?"

"It will when I know more about him," said Mr. Milward.

"Then I'll tell you. He's..."

"Wait, Lucille," He put up a long, thin hand. "Before you tell me any more, let me say something that's...that I feel has got to be said."

"I'm listening," she said tranquilly, and sat on a corner of his desk.

He looked at her. His eyes began at her slender ankles and full, crisp skirt; and then her small, neat waist and her lovely bosom, and her beautiful arms and shoulders— and then her warm, creamy neck, her firm chin, her mouth, her small, pretty nose—and then her magnificent eyes. Adjectives for Lucille— how could one find enough, he wondered? Her hair—her beautiful, soft, curling, copper hair. What man was this—this stranger, this Digby Russell, who had claimed her? Nobody in Greenhurst had ever made any headway with Lucille, he remembered. Jeff—perhaps fortunately—had never felt very warmly towards her; he was always on guard beside Roselle, on watch, waiting for the first hint of unkindness, of harshness, of bullying. Lucille—a bully! The fantastic thought brought a smile to Mr. Milward's lips, and then he remembered what he had to say, and grew serious again.

"I'll be brief," he said. "When your Aunt Maggie and I read your news—not about your decision to sell the house, but of your engagement—we were worried, because we felt that you might, perhaps, be making another mistake. We—" he held up a hand for silence, for she was plainly ready to interrupt, "—we thought your leaving the house was a mistake. One first finds ills, and then one looks for remedies. You found the ills, but you didn't wait to discuss possible remedies; you—"

"I waited a year," said Lucille, steadily. "I didn't want to, you know, but I felt I had to wait. When Mother died, I knew I'd had enough of the house—my instinct was to get out of it, and soon. But I didn't; I felt I owed it to the others to—to have a go at staying there. If Mother's money hadn't been in that Trust—if it had come to us instead of going to Aunt Mary...but even if we'd had the money, what was the use? Roselle wanted to get to London; Nicholas gave no sign of wanting to come back to Greenhurst; the boys seemed perfectly happy about going to live with Aunt Mary. Julia...Julia was the only one who showed any sign of wanting to stay in the house, but I told her that we'd let it for a year, and if she had any complaints, she could let me have them as and when they arose. She's said nothing; she goes to London for holidays with Roselle and I've told her that when I'm married she can come and stay with me." She got off the desk and drew a chair close to her godfather. "Uncle Bill, darling, I know that on paper it looks sad—family breaking up, house being sold, and so on and so on—but it's a great big house and we can't afford servants; Roselle wants a town life and perhaps it'll do her good and bring her out a bit. Nicholas—what is there in Greenhurst for him when he comes out of the Army? Simon and Dominic— are they old enough to have any deep feeling for the house? For myself, I...I had enough. I had nearly eight years of nursing and managing and...and..."

"I understand." He patted her hand gently. "But a year wasn't enough to let you grow to love the house again. And we feel—your Aunt Maggie and I—that you made a mistake in going away. Now we feel that you're running away again— this time from a job that perhaps didn't turn out as well as you hoped..."

There was a question in his voice, and he paused, but Lucille said nothing. Instead, she got up and walked to the window—as Jeff had done earlier that morning—and stood staring out into the street. She had stood there, Mr. Milward remembered, when her head barely came up to the sill; he had had to lift her up to see over the muslin curtain. Now she was tall and could see out for herself...

"Well, my dear?" he asked presently.

"He's a very nice man," said Lucille, without turning, "He's thirty-five—a solicitor; he's not rich, but he's comfortably off. He lives with his mother; she's a widow and he has always lived with her. The house has a nice lot of ground, so when the children come, they can climb trees, and—and run around and—and feel at home."

20

"Where did you meet him?"

"In Bude. The old lady I looked after..." She paused and turned slowly round to face him. "Now *that* was a mistake, if you like," she said. "To go from nursing one frail old lady straight to being a companion to another..."

"But I thought—"

"I know. So did I. You thought from her advertisement that she was a rich, spry old creature who wanted someone to go round the world with her. Willing to travel extensively— that was what she put, wasn't it? When I went to interview her, she said she hadn't been well, but would be up and about soon—then we were going to Paris, and to Rome, and to Florence and to Venice. We were going to Morocco too, and we were going to see her friends in Malta and Colombo and in lovely-sounding places in the South Seas." She came forward and stood looking down at him. "You know, Uncle Bill, I never discovered whether it was all a big swindle, or whether the poor old thing really believed we'd go. I never knew whether it was a plan to trap silly girls into working for her, or whether it was what Nicholas would call a pipe dream. She never got up. She wasn't a difficult patient, like mother; she was quiet and sort of hopeless. I didn't have to nurse her—much; there were plenty of people to help—a housekeeper and two maids and a charwoman and a gardener and a small boy who did odds and ends. It was—you'd say—an easy job—but it wasn't the job I'd hoped it would be. The only extensive travel we ever did was from the house to the sea— eight miles in a hired car once

21

a week in summer. But I never discovered whether she knew—before I came, I mean—that that would be all the travelling we'd do. When I finally realised it, I stayed on because—well, she paid me well and I didn't have much to do—and I couldn't blame her for being ill and not being able to go about...And then I met Digby Russell and things were less dull. He was her solicitor, and he took me out and drove me about and—well, there you are. We got engaged, and then the tenants at Wood Mount went away and I decided to sell the house. So I left my old lady, but before I left, she advertised for my successor in the very same terms. I didn't wait to see her, because I knew I'd have to explain that there wouldn't be any travel, extensive or otherwise. And I still don't know whether it was a trick—or just a hope. But whatever it was, it's over—and here I am."

She stopped, and Mr. Milward rose to his feet almost as though he were about to propose a toast to her happy future. Instead, he looked at her a little sadly.

"When are you going to be married?" he asked.

"In about two months—in Cornwall. Digby's mother felt she couldn't make the journey all the way here for the wedding."

"I wish you sounded as though you knew what you were doing," he said gently. "I know you very well, Lucille, my dear, and I recognise some—I might say most of your moods. This man you mean to marry...of course, one can't judge without having met him—"

"He's very nice. Jeff says he's probably the meek sort,

because I'm a woman who attracts the meek sort."

"Jeff was teasing you."

"No, he wasn't; he thinks I should have persuaded Roselle to stay in Greenhurst and marry him. Try it yourself, Uncle Bill; try persuading a soft, gentle little thing like Roselle once she's got her mind really made up about something. I think—now—that perhaps she might have had some idea of being independent and getting herself off my shoulders—but it's too late to worry about that now. If Jeff couldn't persuade her to stay here and marry him, what makes him think I could have done?"

"Lucille, you're getting angry."

He saw her pause to get her rising temper under control. Perhaps she was not red-haired for nothing, he mused with some sadness; that burnished head was the reflection of the fire within—the heat that moved her to swift and unweighed action, that had driven her out of her home, and now was, perhaps, driving her into this unknown man's arms. Perhaps it was a good thing; marriage might settle her—and if, in marrying, she could unite the family once more down in Cornwall, all might yet turn out to be for the best.

"I'd like to go out and see the house," she said.

"Now—before lunch?"

"If Jeff wouldn't mind taking me."

"Of course he won't mind." Mr. Milward pressed a bell on his desk and sent his stout little secretary to summon Jeff.

23

"You'll see a difference in the place—they loved it, those two old people, and they looked after it well; I didn't like to see them go."

Jeff drove the four miles that separated Wood Mount from the small town of Greenhurst. The road was quiet and almost deserted; Greenhurst was a compact place and did not run to suburbs, at least on this side. With the last of the houses came almost at once broad, open country, dipping beyond Greenhurst and then rising to the wooded slope that gave the house its name. There was a farmhouse or two to be seen on their way, but for the rest, the scene was quiet, green—even, perhaps, uninteresting. But Jeff, glancing at Lucille as he drove, saw that she was looking round with a gaze which—in anybody else—he would have called hungry.

She had changed a little, he thought. She was quieter—less sure of herself, and that was decidedly a change for the better. She was, he had to admit, strikingly beautiful; he had forgotten—or perhaps, engrossed in Roselle as he had been for years, he had not noticed what a beauty Lucille was; he had seen her, chiefly, as a somewhat obstructing elder sister. Striving to be just, he told himself that she had never done or said anything to influence Roselle—that is, she had done nothing to...to put her off him; on the other hand, a word or two in his favour might have helped....It was difficult to say. Greenhurst was a dull sort of place and he himself a dull sort of fellow—and perhaps after her Convent upbringing, Roselle might have experienced some kind of reaction that drove her to leave Wood Mount and go to London. But London...and Roselle—the two didn't go.

But Roselle had gone. He had asked her to marry him—on a Sunday afternoon in summer, just a year ago. He had put it, no doubt, rather bluntly—but things were breaking up before his eyes and he had been driven by a sense of urgency. Lucille was already talking of giving up the house—one was going here, one there; he wanted to keep Roselle. But she had refused to stay; she had refused his offer and turned her back on Greenhurst, and she had gone off to London—and for the first four months she had written: quiet little letters, soft and sweet, like herself. Then she had written no more, and he was left to make of that what he could. London was a busy place—a gay place; a girl could lead a full life there and forget stodgy places...Roselle...

It would be natural, he thought, to ask how she was. Rounding three more curves of the road in order to get the right casualness into his tone, he put the question.

"How's Roselle?"

Lucille turned to look at him in astonishment.

"Don't you know?"

"How should I know? She doesn't write."

"Roselle doesn't write? She didn't tell me she'd—"

"—stopped writing to me? Well, she has. She did. How's she doing?"

"She's still in the same job—with that travel agency.

She's still in the same flat, too. She doesn't tell me much when she writes—she writes regularly, but...I don't know how it is, she doesn't...she doesn't seem to come through in her letters. They're sort of impersonal—they read sometimes like a London Letter column in the Greenhurst rag. But she's well. Julia stayed with her at Easter."

Julia, thought Jeff, with a smile. The other family redhead; the family rebel. The ugly duckling. How old was she now? Simon was eleven, Dominic nine and she came between them; that made her ten. Julia—ten!

"How're the boys?" he asked.

"Nicholas is out of the Army, I think—at least, he wrote to say he was coming out, but he gave me no dates."

"What's he going to do?"

"As little as possible, he says." Lucille sighed. "How does one get jobs for young men?"

"He'll find one for himself. Any news of Simon and Dominic?"

"Very little—you know the kind of letter boys of that age write? Dominic says nothing and Simon says next to nothing. Aunt Mary says they're well and happy and getting good reports at school. When I'm married, I'm going to see about getting them down to Cornwall as often as possible. Your father thought I ought to have written to Aunt Mary about them when she produced the baby— but I wasn't in a position to offer them a home. Now that I am, I want to see about a decent

Prep, school for Dominic and a decent public school, later on, for them both."

An obliging gent, this husband-to-be, reflected Jeff; he was going to be a husband and home provider and residential hotel all in one.

Perhaps Lucille read his thoughts. She said:

"Some men mightn't take on a ready-made family, but I made it clear before I—"

Jeff grinned. He had—so often, so often—heard Lucille making things clear.

"Well, I hope he's a good guy; he sounds it." he said. "What's he look like?"

And that, thought Lucille, was the trouble. He looked... she fought the memory back, but it welled up obstinately, and she remembered it with shame. The first time she had met him, she had thought: Tame rabbit. But she had, as usual, judged too swiftly and too harshly. He had been with his mother in the Vicarage drawing-room, handing round scones and sponge cake—any man in that position would have looked... would have given a wrong impression. But even then, he had been kind and gentle and protective. Later, he had listened patiently when she had talked of her family. He had been audience, sympathiser; he had taken her out of the dullness of life with her untravelling old lady and he had—finally—placed his heart and his house at her disposal. He—

"What happens to his mother?" Jeff broke into her musing. "You said he had an old mother, didn't you?"

"She'll live with us. At least, we're going to live with her."

"Ah. How'll she like Julia and Simon and Dominic?"

"Why shouldn't she like them?"

"Keep your wool on; I didn't say she wouldn't, and you know it. Don't let's pick another quarrel, Lucille. I daresay it'll work out; if she's a nice old lady, they'll cheer her up; if she's a nasty old girl, they'll kill her off. Well—here we are."

He turned into the short drive and Wood Mount stood before them in all its white loveliness.

They got out in silence. Jeff took the key from his pocket and ushered Lucille into the hall; once inside, he gave a glance at her face and then, hands in pockets, wandered away, whistling softly and tunelessly, and left her to roam through the shuttered rooms.

He went into the garden, sat on the low wall of the terrace and, lighting a cigarette, looked thoughtfully at the lovely old house. A long time later, Lucille came out and sat beside him and stared, as he was staring, at the place in which she had been born and reared.

Ghosts, ghosts and more ghosts. Her mother in the library, which overlooked the magnificent holly hedge that she had loved—the hedge that took two men two months to trim. Her father in his old study. Herself in the old day nursery, from the window of which she had watched the slow growth of Dominic's...she pulled herself up sharply. Enough of that.

It took a fool to make a wise decision and then look round for reasons to regret it. All that stuff up there in the attics—her father's, her mother's, her own, Nicholas's, Roselle's, Julia's, the boys'...stirring up old memories, old scenes, old dreams...

"Well?" said Jeff, at last.

"I suppose living in a place all your life makes you kind of...take it for granted," said Lucille slowly.

"It didn't look like this when you left it, you know. Those tenants put a lot of money into it. When you left here, the garden looked like a fair-ground and the house looked seedy. They took the central heating up to the top of the house and they made that extra bathroom; they cleared out that hell-hole you used to call the summer house; they rebuilt the so-called stables and they made the garage a garage. They wouldn't have done it, mark you, if they'd known they were going back to South Africa at the end of the year. Their idea, from the first, was to buy the place—if you'd sell, and you'd made it pretty clear that you'd probably sell."

"To run it, I'd need money. Where would I have got money?"

"Couldn't you have persuaded your fiancé to come and take it over?"

"No. I thought of it—but it would have been no use asking him—he's tied to his business, and he got his mother to think of. He couldn't leave them—and I don't suppose he'd want to. No...it'll have to go, Jeff."

"Any regrets?"

"Yes."

"Then why not let it again? Take more time to think—give it another year."

"What's the use? We'll all be down in Cornwall by that time. If Nicholas....if only he'd been older, if only he'd met an heiress, if only he could have..."

She stopped, staring up at the house. Something in her silence struck Jeff and, turning to her, he stiffened in surprise. There were tears on her cheeks—and although he had seen her cry, not once but many times, he had never seen her cry like this. She had wept from temper, from weariness, from exasperation—but this quiet, gentle melancholy was something different. To his own astonishment, he found himself grasping one of her hands and patting it awkwardly. Fatherly, that's what, he thought confusedly. There-there and come-come.

Lucille...in need of comfort! The assured, overriding, I'll-fix-it-all Lucille Wayne...groping for a handkerchief and hanging on to the nearest support— himself. This was where he ought to whip out a clean square of linen and mop her up—but he'd used his handkerchief to clean up his hands after a grope round the carburettor. All he could do was look sympathetic and wait for her to pull herself together.

"Feeling better?" he asked at last.

She nodded.

"Yes, thank you." She blew her nose; a loud, defiant blast

sounded in the ear of fate. "What did you put in the advertisement?"

"I've got it here somewhere," said Jeff, fishing. "Here: For Sale, desirable Residence, four miles from market town; colonial style, wooded grounds, extensive views. Hall, four recep., ten bed, two bath..."

"That, I think," broke in Lucille dreamily, "is really what went wrong—at the end, I mean, with Mother. When she came here, I think she saw herself as a—a chatelaine—a tall, gracious figure moving about the house or through the grounds with a troop of delightful children at her heels, and—"

"Well, the picture's substantially correct: she was tall and gracious and she certainly had a troop of children."

"Yes—but in her imagination, I know just how it must have been—at first. She had that kind of romantic, unpractical, out-of-this-life imagination like—" she stopped on the brink of adding 'like Roselle', and went on: "She saw herself *presiding*—sitting quietly in the centre of everything and directing the servants. There must have been a lot of servants—in her imagination. This house looks like one of those old plantation ones, and she imagined an old housekeeper and a gentle, fatherly old butler—and the lesser ones a sort of Deep South collection, only with white faces instead of black ones. She probably pictured a governess, too—a *Ma'mselle*, small and spry and sharp, rounding us all up and seeing that we talked French in the schoolroom. That's the kind of place it was—as Mother saw it. And how did it turn out, in real, cold, hard

31

life? The house was too big, and too rambling and much too large to heat inexpensively; the servants were two in number and decrepit; the children were a troop all right, but a noisy, disorderly troop. And she herself couldn't sit around directing graciously; she had to be up and doing—and she wasn't a doer, you know, Jeff; God makes the Marthas and the Marys and I forget which was which, but Mother was the one who didn't do the chores. Roselle would have been the same—only she was born into a more practical world. But Mother—And then, of course, Simon and Julia and Dominic came too late; she was forty-six when Dominic was born and those last three were just too much. I don't think it was the work or the worry or the lack of money that made her so...so difficult at the end; I think it was just the thought of how differently things had turned out."

"A lot of people get bitter because they oversell something to themselves. It came hard on you."

"In a way, I suppose. I'll never know whether it formed my character or ruined my temper. How much d'you think we'll get for the house, Jeff?"

"Hard to say; big houses don't fetch much nowadays— and there's no bus service out here. Not more than seven thousand, Dad says. If that. We're asking eight. It isn't remote, but it's a bit, shall we say, cut-off—there's no gas laid on—all that adds up, or should we say subtracts.—Lucille—"

"Well?"

"Have you told the—the others that you're selling?"

32

"Yes."

"What did they say?"

"Nothing—yet. I wrote to them all from Cornwall and... and explained. Or tried to explain. And I asked them to write and let me know which of their things they'd like to keep. Most of the stuff will have to go, of course, but if they could choose..."

"Not everything they'll choose is portable, you know."

"I know, but"—Lucille moved restlessly— "there it is, Jeff. We've all got to accept it, that's all. The letters have gone; they'll know by now."

Jeff said nothing. He wanted to speak—but this was the end. This was finality. There was nothing more to say.

Chapter Two

Lucille's letters usually reached Simon on Saturday mornings. They were beside his plate when he got to the breakfast table, and he could take his time about reading them, for Saturday was the only morning of the week on which he could linger over his food. On other days, he had to eat with one eye on the clock and the other upon Dominic, who was convinced that the school bus would wait for him, even when it had given two unsympathetic demonstrations that it wouldn't. On both these occasions, Simon had been ready to go; he could have gone to school alone—but he had stayed with Dominic, obeying the same dim sense of responsibility that made him, Saturday after Saturday, read Lucille's letter aloud to him, even when it was plain that Dominic's mind was elsewhere.

A year ago, the arrival of any family letter had made something of a stir at the breakfast table. Dominic would clamour to open it; Aunt Mary and Uncle Francis would look up from their toast or their bacon and ask what the news was. There had been plenty of letters and plenty of news to give them: in Lucille's letter from Cornwall, in Roselle's from London and even in Julia's from the Convent. But the months had gone by and the letters had become fewer and progressively more dull; now, Simon's aunt and uncle merely said "Ah, letter from Lucille" and went on with their breakfast. Dominic scarcely listened when they were read to him, and even Simon found himself opening the envelope, glancing hurriedly through the contents and cramming them into his pocket to be read more fully—perhaps—later.

But not this morning's letter from Lucille...

It had found him totally unprepared. When he picked it up and opened it, it had looked no different from Lucille's other correspondence. There was the same notepaper with the same heading; there was the usual greyish-blue envelope. There was about a page and a half, written in Lucille's careless scrawl; Simon had skimmed almost to the end of the first page when it happened—when a faint, undefined feeling of nausea gripped his stomach and the mouthful of buttered toast he was eating turned into sour-tasting dough. He went back to the first line and read it more slowly, right through to the end; then he found that his appetite had left him.

He folded up the letter and put it back in its envelope. Laying it beside his plate, he stared at it for a long time, as though by this means he could discover what there was about it that could have had so upsetting an effect upon his digestion. He could not remember anything in his life that had given him this sick feeling of disaster. He was surprised that his uncle, glancing at him as he asked for the butter, seemed to see nothing unusual about him. His aunt, getting up from the table, issued instructions about the morning's plans and noted nothing out of the ordinary in his expression. It must then, thought Simon, be all inside him; he felt green, but he didn't look green. Further, although his mind was confused, he was able to follow his aunt's directions and to answer them intelligently. "There's nothing else, is there, Simon?"

"I don't think so, Aunt Mary."

"You'll find your lunches in the fridge. If Dominic wants more milk, use the small bottle."

"Yes, Aunt Mary."

"Clear up after you—you needn't wash up, just pile the things neatly. We'll be back in time for tea."

"You will; I won't." It was Uncle Francis's voice. "I shan't be back until about six."

"Well, I'll be back."

"All right, Aunt Mary."

"If there are any phone messages, Simon, write them down yourself, will you? Dominic's hopeless at it—I can never understand what he writes down."

"I'll do them, Aunt Mary."

"Thank you. Go up, will you, and keep the baby quiet for a moment—he's yelling his head off."

Simon went upstairs and stood by the cot; his two-months-old cousin went on howling, but Simon scarcely heard him. Lucille's letter was in his hand and he was reading it through again in the hope of finding his fears groundless. Perhaps Lucille hadn't really meant it...

But the letter was only too clear. There was no mistake; the sentences read just as Lucille would have spoken them—they were clear, decisive and quite, quite final, for Lucille spoke not merely as an older sister, but also as a guardian. She was, he knew, the one who ordered all their lives; that is, amended Simon, staring at the baby, his life, Julia's and Dominic's. Nicholas was grown up; Roselle was eighteen and could decide for herself; she had decided for herself, and now she was living in London. But Julia was only ten, and she and Dominic and himself—the three young ones—had always obeyed Lucille.

For the first time, Simon groped for and found a word that had always eluded him when he thought of his family. Untidy. That was it—untidy. Other families were in a bunch, tidy, compact, more or less of an age. But look at his own family; Simon, looking at it with eyes full of misery, saw it sprawling untidily, unevenly and acknowledged that it was a difficult one to keep together. At one end, Lucille; then Nicholas and Roselle; then a gap—a yawning chasm and on the other side of it himself, Julia and Dominic. It wasn't any wonder, thought Simon, that they had come apart; it was only a wonder that they stayed together for so long...for all his life, until just a year ago. Perhaps he had been expecting too much, hoping too much, when he had looked forward with such confidence to a reunion; perhaps he shouldn't have been surprised this morning when he read what Lucille had said.

Final words; shattering words. The howls of the baby

were no more than an echo of the desolation that filled Simon's heart.

He went into the bedroom he shared with Dominic and stood by the window listening to the familiar Saturday-morning sounds. His thin, brown face with its perpetually harassed look that was caused by the weight of responsibility he always felt for Julia and Dominic, now looked strained, old beyond his years. He heard his uncle leaving the house. His aunt came upstairs, the baby stopped crying. Dominic called from the garden, but Simon stood where he was.

Later, his aunt left to spend the day with a friend and took the baby with her. The charwoman made a brief appearance, went through the motions of sweeping and dusting, washed up the breakfast things, broke two saucers and departed noisily. With her going, peace descended upon the house and Simon and Dominic were left alone. But this fact, which as a rule brought Simon a great deal of pleasure and relief, was to-day overshadowed by the news in Lucille's letter. His mind was filled with only one thought: to go to Dominic and read it aloud to him—for if Dominic, after listening, showed no sign of surprise or alarm, it would mean that this sick feeling was caused by needless worry; that it had all been a fuss over nothing; that all was well. Dominic lived in a world of his own, far removed from the worries and inconveniences of everyday life— but he came back very promptly when his interests were threatened. Other people might worry all the time—but Dominic could pick, unerringly, the real trouble from a thousand imagined ones. Dominic would listen now, and Dominic would know.

Dominic was where his brother expected him to be: up a tree in the garden. After an attempt at making him come down, Simon decided to go up. He was an expert climber, but he remembered, as he left the ground, that he hadn't done much climbing in the past year. A year ago, he had spent almost as much time aloft as aground—but then they had all been at home, and at home there were a great many more trees. Nicholas had taught them—Simon and Julia and Dominic—the best way to climb them. He had rigged up a hammock for Julia under the shadiest apple tree. He had helped Dominic to build his magnificent tree house. The tree house...What would happen to the tree-house now? And where would Julia find a place where she could read, hour by hour, quiet and undisturbed? Where...but this, decided Simon, pulling himself up mentally and physically, this was fussing over nothing. He would ask Dominic. If Dominic didn't feel anything, didn't sense anything, then it would mean that the future was safe and clear.

He reached the branch on which Dominic sat, and with a spring and a twist, settled beside him.

"'lo," said Dominic.

Simon, glancing at him, was struck, as he had been struck so often before, by a feeling of regret that Dominic and the others were so good-looking while Julia was so ugly. He never agreed—audibly—when people said that she was ugly, but he acknowledged to himself that she did have a rather monkeyish sort of face and somewhat stringy red hair, and he had to admit that she looked even worse in the summer, when her freckles came out. It seemed a shame that Dominic should have the fair, clear skin and the big, grey eyes and the almost girlish lashes.

He looked away from Dominic and studied the view below them. The garden, seen from up here, seemed bigger; the neighbouring houses looked less over-shadowing. Above, the June sun shone; beside him, Dominic hummed a tuneless little air. Simon felt a little better. He needed only Dominic's "Pooh, of *course* she won't" to restore him to cheerfulness.

He began by diving a hand into his pocket and bringing out Lucille's letter. It was badly crushed and one or two of the words had been obliterated, but Simon knew it all by memory. Now he could put it to the test.

"Shall I read you the letter from Lucille?"

Dominic had swung backwards and was now hanging upside-down by his knees. He groped to an upright position and screwed himself round to examine, with interest but no anxiety, a part of his trousers that had got torn during the operation.

"'Tisn't much," he reported. "Anyhow, it's an old pair."

"Didn't you hear what I said? I said shall I read you Lucille's letter?"

Dominic's large, beautiful grey eyes rested indifferently on his brother for a moment.

"If you like," he said.

With this encouragement, Simon balanced himself precariously and smoothed out the letter on his knee.

"Shall I read it, or tell you about it?"

"Tell me about it."

"Well...it's a sort of funny letter this time. Lucille says— *Dominic,* I'm *telling* you something."

Dominic, upside down once more, was swinging to and fro with a skill that would have won him a place in any circus, and caused the death of any weak-hearted observer.

"*Dominic!*"

Dominic, reappearing, shook his hair out of his eyes. "I bet Julia can't do that. She tried to do it before, when we were at home, and she couldn't. I bet I do it better than her."

"Will you listen to what I'm telling you?"

"What about?"

"About Lucille."

"Go on, then."

"She's getting married, and—"

"Look," interrupted Dominic, pointing a grubby forefinger; "You can see right into the nursery from here. I can see the baby's cot, can't you?"

"Are you going to listen or aren't you?"

"I did listen. I heard what you said. Lucille's going to get married. What's funny about that? When you're as old as that, I shouldn't be s'prised if you got married."

"But don't you *remember?* Lucille said that after a year,

41

we could go home again. She'd let the house for a year, she said. Those people took it for a year, and Lucille said that after a year they'd go away and she'd come back from Cornwall and we'd all go home and five at home again—if we wanted to."

"Well, all right," said Dominic, calmly. "Tell her we want to."

"But I'm trying to *explain*. Lucille's going to get married, she says, and—those people have gone away and the house is....Simon stopped, swallowed and concluded his explanation. "It's going to be sold."

"Well, it can't be," stated Dominic flatly and without hesitation, "'cos we're all going back there."

Simon sat for some moments weighing his fears against a feeling of relief. The certainty in Dominic's voice bore out the confidence that he himself had felt regarding their eventual return home. He tried to put himself back to the time when the fate of the house had first been in doubt, and found his memories hazy almost to vanishing point. It was two years ago. He could remember their mother's funeral—he and Julia had been told to keep Dominic out of the way, and the three of them had had a very good view of the procession from the window of the second floor bathroom. After that, they had stayed on at Wood Mount for a year, and then Lucille had called a family meeting, and told them all about her plan to let the house for a year. He had tried to understand all the financial details that she had written down on a piece of paper; he had even tried to put forward his point of view as lucidly as Nicholas had voiced his—but they were old enough to understand, while he...

It seemed to Simon, looking back, that there had never really been more than one possible end to the discussion. They could not afford to go on living in the house, and so the sole choice had lain between selling it or letting it; they had let it, in the end, for a year. So much came back to him, but when he went further, when he tried to remember what had been planned for the year's end, he could recall nothing more definite than Lucille's hurriedly given assurance that they might all go back. If they wanted to, she had said. In the meantime, she was going to travel with an old lady and look after her. She was going to France, Italy and places like that—places she had always wanted to go to—where she would have gone before if father hadn't got ill—and then, later, if mother had not become ill. Roselle was to go to London, and work there. Nicholas was away, and so he couldn't say anything. Julia... well, Simon remembered, Julia hadn't really wanted to go anywhere. Julia had wanted to stay at home, just as he and Dominic had wanted to stay at home. He and Dominic hadn't been insistent, and Julia had—but nobody had really listened to Julia; nobody could take advice, he supposed, from a girl of nine, as she had been then—and nobody was going to agree to give up a good year's let and stay in the house just because Julia had three hundred and five books in it. It had seemed, then, a silly reason for staying. Now...somehow, it didn't look so silly. It was one thing for her books to be stored in the attic for a year—but if Lucille sold the house, where could the books be put? They wouldn't fit into Roselle's flat in London, poky hole that it was. His aunt and uncle wouldn't agree to having them here. Then where else was there? Lucille's new home...but would her husband want Julia's books? And if Julia's books had to go, where would Dominic's tree-house go? What would happen to it? It had taken them—Julia and Dominic and himself, with Nicholas's help—nearly ten months to build. Even Lucille and Roselle had helped, and Nicholas had carried up the heavy bits, and it had been built firmly and solidly in the great oak tree. They had spent days—long days—in it. Dominic hadn't spoken much of home, in this last year, but whenever he did, it was his tree house that he spoke of.

And for himself...if he had known, thought Simon, if he had dreamed that it would be more than a year...but when they sat in the library that evening and Lucille had explained that there was no money to live in the house, that he and Dominic were to go and live with Uncle Francis and Aunt Mary and make their home with them, it had been—he was sure it had been for a year only, until they could see how much money there was...Perhaps he hadn't been listening properly because he had been thinking of— of—well, he'd better keep his mind off that now, or the feeling in his inside would get worse, and he couldn't really be sick properly up in a tree.

Things couldn't be as bad as he was making out, or Dominic would have shown some signs of alarm, instead of stating calmly and definitely, that they were all going back home. But—

"Perhaps I'd better read you the letter," he told Dominic.

"You've told me all what's in it."

"No—only partly. Lucille's getting married and she's going to live in Cornwall, she says. And she's taking some things and the rest is going to be sold."

"*Our* things—sold?" Dominic turned to stare at him, for the first time giving the matter his full attention.

"Well, yes," said Simon. "Not our *things*; just the furniture, like chairs and tables and beds and things."

"Then what about our things? What about all our stuff up in the attics?" demanded Dominic.

"That's what Lucille wants to know. She says she's going home to sort everything out—she's at home now; she arrives there to-day to sign papers and things about the house so's people can come and buy it, and she's going to stay there for a bit to—to clear up everything—and she says we're to write to her and tell her which of our things we want."

Dominic was still staring at him, and his eyes were wide open now, and—to Simon's relief—full of interest.

Dominic was listening—really listening—and that in itself, in any way, was a danger signal.

"How do you mean—which of our things?" demanded Dominic.

"That's what Lucille says—she says we've got to write at once, because she'll be staying at the house. Then when it's all done, she's coming to see us and, perhaps, bringing Digby."

45

"Digby? What's Digby?"

"*Who*. Digby's a man—that one she's going to get married to."

"Well, but what about our things?" said Dominic, glancing off lesser matters.

"I've told you. Lucille says we've to decide what we want out of it all, and tell her and she'll see we get them."

"See we *get* them?" Dominic's eyes narrowed, and Simon saw in them incredulity and the beginning of anger. "See we *get* them? How d'you mean, see we *get* them? They're *ours*, aren't they?" Dominic's voice rose. "We've *got* them. We've got them at home. What's she think she's going to do—chuck out all our things just because some silly fatheads go and say they want to buy our house?"

"Nobody said anything about chucking them out. All you've got to do, she says, is to tell her what you want, and she'll see you get it."

"All right, then," said Dominic triumphantly. "I want my tree house—see? Tell her to send me *that*—''

"She can't do that."

"'course she can't, and that's why she's talking tripe—see?" explained Dominic. "She can't send me my tree house, can she, and she can't send Julia her books, can she,, all three hundred and five of the great, thumping things, can she, and she can't send you Long John because they won't let you have your dog here—see?"

It was said. The name was spoken.

For a whole year, Simon had kept his resolve. For a whole year, he had kept the name of Long John hidden away, deep, deep inside him. Never once had he mentioned him. And as Dominic had never spoken of him, as Julia had never written of him, he had assumed that they had forgotten. Now he saw that Dominic had not forgotten, and that Julia, too, must remember. Nobody could forget how he, Simon, had saved Long John's life and carried him home—an eight-weeks puppy—and nursed him until he was well and strong and scampering round the house on his three and a half legs. Nobody could forget how he, Simon, had laboured, long and patiently, to teach Long John the mysteries of life—for the van which had left him half a leg short had also been responsible for rattling his brains a little out of place, so that there were certain things— things that came naturally to other dogs—that Long John had to learn: how to come downstairs, for example. It was no use his thinking that he could take off at the top and just float down. How to bury a bone; it was no use his going off to find the ideal burying-ground and then going all the way back to fetch the bone, because the cat liked bones too, and always got there first—and even if the bone had still been there, Long John wouldn't have been able to locate it, because he could only smell the smell-before-last. People laughed at Long John—until they got to know him, and they stopped laughing, because they discovered he had what Nicholas called an unusual personality. And he had definite likes

47

and dislikes which, of course, all dogs did—but what dog, except Long John, would get hold of all the things belonging to a visitor he didn't care for, and carry them and put them outside the front door, just as a hint? What other dog could sing duets, or chase two separate rabbits in two separate directions—both at once? What other dog, if it came to that, ever looked like Long John? Most people could say what kind a dog was even if it was more than one kind of dog—but Long John kept them all guessing, and even old Mr. Hewett himself, who had bought him out of a Pet Shop window because he said something came over him—even Mr. Hewett, who knew all about dogs, couldn't settle upon Long John's ancestry. A sheep dog coat, a bull terrier chest, a noble Great Dane head and a long, bushy banner of a tail waving behind....

Long John. Did dogs forget, in a year? Mr. Hewett had said they didn't, and he had promised to talk to Long John about Simon, and to say his name and to keep him up to his painfully-acquired tricks. But a year...a whole year! Would he remember, after so long at Mr. Hewett's farm, which was his real and which was his temporary home? Would he understand that Simon had wanted so desperately to bring him here, and couldn't? There was not much room here, inside or out. And if he had come, he would have had to go away when the baby was born, because Simon's aunt said that she wouldn't mix dogs and babies.

If Lucille was going to sell the house, were he and Dominic to live here, with their aunt and uncle, for ever and ever?

Would Nicholas go on being a soldier? Did Roselle really want to leave home for ever and stay in that poky flat in that noisy street in London? And Julia...Julia hadn't really got any home. It had been arranged that she would spend her Christmas holidays with Roselle in London and her summer holidays here in this house—but the summer holidays would begin in three weeks and the room which, last year, had been Julia's, was now the nursery and the baby was in it. Surely Lucille knew? Didn't she understand? But if she was going to be married and live in Cornwall, people, Simon remembered with a stab of fear, people didn't as a rule cart their whole family when they got married. And if there still wasn't enough money to live at home—

Money! It all came down, came back to money. Their father, Lucille had said, had once had some money, but it had all got spent. His mother had had some money, quite a lot of money, Lucille said, but it was all in what they called a Trust, and when she died, it went to her sister, Aunt Mary, and that was why Aunt Mary had offered to have Dominic and himself to live with her. But Lucille hadn't said it would be for ever! She had said that they would try it for a year.

Simon's memory of his mother was still vivid, but of his father he remembered nothing. He could not remember having missed his parents—but now, for the first time, he felt a new and great need for a father or mother to whom he could appeal against Lucille's decree. He was aware, for his mother had told him again and again, that his father had loved the house; he had loved it, she said, almost better than anything else in the world. It was a lovely house and round it were lovely grounds and in it they had all been united and happy. It couldn't...it couldn't happen, now, that strangers would buy it and live in it while they—Lucille and Nicholas and Roselle and Julia and himself and Dominic—who had been born in it, brought up in it, had to live in places they didn't want to live in. It wasn't possible and it couldn't happen...but in his hands was a letter which stated that it was more than possible. It was going to happen.

A rush of nausea shook Simon and he turned to Dominic. "I'm going down," he said.

"No." said Dominic, "Wait. You haven't said anything."

"Yes, I have. I've told you what Lucille said."

"Well, I don't care what Lucille said."

Dominic's voice had the calm matter-of-factness that Simon so envied. Dominic never wasted a thought on any-body else's point of view; he stated his own, and if anybody disagreed with him, he assumed that they had not heard him properly, and said it all over again. He was not, now, being defiant; he really didn't care what Lucille said; Lucille was free to say anything she liked, but he, Dominic, was going to have his say, too.

"Lucille's our guardian," Simon pointed out. "If she says anything has to happen, then it has to."

"Rot," said Dominic firmly. "Tommy-rot and tripe. It isn't

all her house—it's our house, too. She told me so, once. It's our house as well as hers, and she can't do anything on her own without asking us."

"Yes, she can. We're minors."

"We're what?"

"We're sort of too young, and we don't have a say."

"Oh, don't we?" enquired Dominic. "Well, *I* do. And I'm going to say I want to go home. She said we'd come here for a year, and the year's up; all right, we go home—see?"

"Don't be silly."

"What's silly?" asked Dominic in genuine surprise. "She won't know what we want unless we tell her, will she? How does she know we want to go home unless we *tell* her?"

"But she says the sale's practically arranged."

"What sale?"

"I've told you—the sale of the house. All you have to do is sign some papers, and then people buy it and pay for it, and then it'll be theirs."

The steady patience, and some other quality—something of desperation in his voice brought Dominic's gaze round to rest on him once more, and this time, the grey eyes were cool and calculating.

"Those people," he asked, "where are they?"

"Which people?"

"Those ones who want to buy the house."

"There's nobody special yet. Whoever wants it will go

51

and look at it and then if they like it, they'll buy it."

"Then where'll Lucille be?"

"She'll be there, but only for a few days, she says."

"You mean she'll be in the house by herself?"

"Yes."

"Not those other people."

"No. Not yet."

"Oh. How much," went on Dominic without the slightest pause, "have you got in your purse?"

"My *purse*? What's my purse got to do with it?"

"Well, how much have you got in it?"

"I think one pound six...no, seven shillings."

"How much have I got in my money box?"

"About two pounds, last time you asked me to look."

"Is that enough—two pounds and one pound six—to get home on?"

"*Home* on?" Simon could only echo the words stupidly. "*Home* on?"

"What's it cost to go from here to there in a train?"

"Don't be silly," said Simon with what, for him, was sharpness. "We'd never be allowed."

"Of course not," agreed Dominic calmly, "but they'd never know. I mean, not till we'd gone."

"If you tried to do anything like that, why, all they'd have to do would be to ring up all the stations we stopped at from here to London, and they'd get us out of the train and send us back."

"No, they wouldn't. We're not like *Uncle Tom's Cabin*. We'll just go, and we'll leave a letter on the hall table and say not to worry, and Lucille'll ring up when we get home and tell them we're there with her, and then it'll be all right and we can talk to her and tell her about not selling the house to any other people."

It was spoken with such coolness, such confidence, such certainty, that Simon could find nothing to say. The more he studied the scheme, the more reasonable it seemed. They were doing nothing sensational; they were not running away. They were not even going away without permission; it was simply that they could not stop to ask for sanction; they had to go at once. Time was a vital factor, because Lucille was not going to be at home long. And in any case, this was not the moment for stopping to wonder what their aunt and uncle might think; it was only necessary to stop and consider what would happen if he and Dominic *didn't* go home. They had to see Lucille— see her, talk to her, convince her that she was acting against all their interests. If they didn't get to her to-day, if they stayed here, doing nothing, Lucille would act. She would act, and their home—their only home—would be sold and life—real life—would be over. Living here was all very well as a temporary arrangement, but for ever and ever...No! This wasn't the time to argue or debate or shillyshally. Dominic had the right idea, which was to get there. If they waited it would be too late.

"We could take our lunch with us and eat it in the bus on the way to Shrewsbury to catch a train," said Dominic.

From Shrewsbury, they could get a train to London. They could cross London and catch a train to Greenhurst— they had done the journey up here and all they had to do was reverse the order.

Greenhurst...they would be four miles from home when they reached the familiar little station. Greenhurst...and from Greenhurst they could get a bus a little way and walk the rest.

Home!

It was breathtakingly bold. It was revolutionary. It was the first step in lawlessness....But it would lead them home.

"Well, are you coming?" asked Dominic.

"I'm...Yes." said Simon.

"Well then, why don't we go?"

Simon stared out through the branches, over the trees in the neighbouring gardens and to a far distant point on the sky-line. A huge, shaggy head and—at the other end— a banner waving.

"Come on," he said. "Careful; I'll go down first."

Chapter Three

Julia read the letter at the end of a compulsory cricket practice which she had found—as she found all games—very boring. Saturday was, on the whole, she considered, a gruesome day. Laundry-sorting day, cricket-practice day, long-walk day, letter-writing and choir-practice day. Gruesome, all of it.

It was something to have a regular letter to look forward to, though Nicholas and Roselle scarcely ever wrote now, and Lucille's letters had got pretty dull lately, and scarcely worth the trouble and eye-strain involved in deciphering them. Who cared about Bodmin or Bude or Boscastle? If they were anything like London, they could have them; how anybody could *live* in gruesome places like London, with people pushing you everywhere, and houses stuck close together, and entire herds of people crammed into one building, was more than she could understand. If people had to live there, then they had to, but it was difficult to understand why Roselle chose to; she could have stayed close to home and worked in a Greenhurst office, even if it was less money—and if she had done that, she, Julia could have gone there for holidays instead of stuffing in

Roselle's flat or being palmed off on to Aunt Mary, who didn't want her. Roselle's flat...a gruesome camp bed in that ghastly box of a room in what—before she had seen it— Julia had presumed to be a decent flat that decent people could live in.

Life, on the whole, was terrible, and if one couldn't get away from it and read, and read, and read...Oh well, now there was Lucille's letter to read.

Julia read it.

Long, long after she had got to the last scrawled line, she looked up and found, to her surprise, that the fat Belinda Grant, who had brought the letter all the way out to the Games field, was still standing beside her. She stared for a moment, and then realised that Belinda hadn't, after all, been there very long. It was only that she herself had been—in that brief time—a long, long way away. It had only been a few moments, but they had been long enough for her to go home and back.

"Can I have the stamp?" asked Belinda.

"Here." Julia tore off a corner of the envelope and held it out.

"Is that your sister's letter?" went on Belinda, whose ruling passion was a desire to find out all about everybody.

"Yes."

"What's she say?"

"Nothing."

"Then what's the use of writing?"

"You mind your own business," requested Julia, fiercely.

Belinda's eyes opened wide in surprise. Julia Wayne was credited with a great many faults, but—in spite of her red hair—bad temper was not among them.

"I didn't say anything—I just said ' What's the use of writing, if you don't say anything '. That's nothing to snap at, I wouldn't say."

Julia let the matter drop. There was something on her mind that was more important than bickering. She had put Lucille's letter back into what remained of the envelope and pushed it into the pocket of her tunic. She always put the letters into her pocket after a hasty reading, and usually she forgot them immediately—but this morning, it seemed to her that she could still see the words: they were written on Belinda's face, on the cricket bat lying on the grass, and they were written, not in the blue-black ink that Lucille had used, but in bright red letters. A warning, thought Julia; a warning that something terrible was going to happen.

Nothing was clear in her mind. She felt as she had done in the dentist's chair, when she had seen the dentist put out his foot to start the drilling-machine—or as she had felt when preparations were going forward for the removal of her tonsils. Her mouth was full of saliva; she swallowed, and more came.

"Come on," said Belinda, "They've put out the milk and biscuits."

"You go. I don't want any."

"Why don't you?"

57

"You *go*, I said!" repeated Julia, fiercely.

Belinda went, wondering, as she did so, why she called Julia her best friend. There were plenty of others, she recalled, who were only too ready to be her best friend, and why she stuck to Julia was a puzzle. She glanced back: Julia was still standing where she had left her, staring into space. She might say that her sister had said nothing, but it was ten to one she'd written her a few hard words on how many bad marks she'd got last month for reading— not reading in class, or reading the proper school books, but for reading in bed, in Chapel, or under her desk during the French lessons. Julia wasn't the boasting type, one had to give her that, but she did rather harp on the three-hundred and what-was-it books she had at home up in the attic. She'd never thrown a single book away in her whole life, not even her baby books; some of them even had teeth marks on them. She was mad on books, which was silly, because goodness knows, you got enough books at school and it was crazy to sit and read when you could be playing games. Julia only played games when they were compulsory, like cricket. The rest of the time, she just read, curled up anywhere, looking—a lot of the girls said—like a studious monkey. It was true that Julia wasn't pretty, but somehow, her small monkeyish face suited her; at least, she wasn't like anybody else. That was the reason why it was nice to take her home every fourth Saturday, when they were allowed to sleep at home for two nights.

They all liked Julia, at home; they said it was because

she was a homeless orphan and they were sorry for her, but it wasn't that, because Julia wasn't the pathetic type. The real reason that all grown-ups liked her was because she wasn't shy or sugary, like girls—she was more like a boy; she answered people in a sort of direct, natural way, without trying to make an impression. She could make an impression if she liked, but she never did try; she even went out of her way to make the nuns angry, and some of her Reports were worth framing for the things they wrote about her.

Eleven o'clock: milk and biscuits. She might as well take two shares and say she'd take one lot to Julia; nobody'd know that Julia didn't want any, and she herself was starving. This school didn't really feed people properly.

It was just like that interfering poke-nose of a Sister Ignatius to go by just as she'd started on the second lot of biscuits. Oh, well...

"Why didn't you take them to Julia?"

"Well, I did ask, Sister, but she said she wasn't hungry."

"Where is she?"

"At the nets, Sister."

"Does she not feel well?"

Belinda, on the point of saying that only ill-health could account for Julia's unusual behaviour, remembered that this would lead to her friend's being forbidden to go home with her for the week-end.

"She feels all right, I think, Sister. She just didn't feel like milk and biscuits."

"Send her to me, please."

Julia, summoned, ate her mid-morning refreshment meekly. This school was always stuffing things down you, like pigs to market. And asking silly questions.

"Did you have a letter from Lucille this morning?"

"Yes, Sister."

"I hope everything is all right."

"Yes, thank you, Sister."

"Is there any special news?"

No monkey ever looked blanker.

"No, Sister."

"Are your brothers well?"

"Yes, thank you, Sister."

"Did you hear from them?"

"No, Sister."

"How is Roselle?"

Yes, of course, that had to come, thought Julia. They always wanted to know how Roselle was. Roselle was every school's idea of the perfect pupil: pretty as a flower, with gentle manners and a sweet smile and a disposition like plasticine that they could mould into prefects and head girls and showpieces, and get heaps of new pupils because their stupid mothers thought that all their children would turn out like Roselle. Roselle...who, at eighteen, had deliberately chosen, of her own free will, to leave a home that was perfection; Roselle, who now stewed all day in a silly Travel office in London and then went home—home, pah!—at night to a beastly room and a share of hundreds of other people's bathroom and a gruesome smell of cabbage all over the place. Roselle, the London career girl. Well, she could have it. Never, never, never again would she, Julia, sleep on that camp bed and go five times up those stairs to the bathroom before being able to get inside it. Never. She'd rather go to Aunt Mary's even if there was a howling baby in the room now. Even Aunt Mary's was poky and noisy enough, goodness knows, compared with home, but it was better than what Roselle called her flat.

"Julia—"

"Yes, Sister?"

Sister Ignatius sighed, and decided that it was no use. Julia Wayne led a life of her own and it was not the life of the school. It was a pity that she was so different from her sister, Roselle. There was a lot in Julia, if one could find out where it was and what it was, but she was—as her sister, Lucille, had expressed it, crudely but vividly, in one of her letters to Mother Superior—not so much a cog in the wheel as a spanner in the works. It was a pity, but she did not seem to fit in here. It was insecurity, of course; no parents, and a young girl of twenty-four at the head of the family. Lucille was, no doubt, quite capable of directing their affairs, but unless she had changed greatly in the last few years, there was no doubt that she was given to too-swift decisions. That was all very well if they were the right decisions, but at twenty-four, and with Lucille's impetuosity, they usually weren't. Julia appeared to be well, and as it was impossible to find out for certain, one could only hope that she was happy. Belinda's parents liked her and frequently invited her down for the month-end visit; perhaps this afternoon, when the big car took the two girls off, Julia would get her colour back—those freckled girls never had much colour—and forget whatever it was in her sister's letter that had given her that curious look in her eyes.

Julia always enjoyed the drive; Belinda's parents sent a car and a chauffeur and a heavy picnic-hamper to sustain the two passengers on the way; the journey, apart from Belinda's too-often-heard voice, was full of the peace and quietness that Julia loved. Belinda saw that her friend's irritation of the morning had gone; Julia was as calm as usual, and only a little more preoccupied, staring through the glass partition at the chauffeur's back and answering her companion's questions absently, and after some prodding.

"Has your brother, Nicholas, finished his National Service yet?"

"I don't know."

"Will you see your other brothers these hols?"

"Who—Simon and Dominic? Yes, I suppose so."

"I thought you were going to Roselle's."

"I don't care for London at this time of the year," said Julia. This kind of car bred that kind of manner.

"Won't Roselle want you, if she's all alone?"

"She may come and stay with my aunt, too. She says she gets two weeks holiday."

Two weeks! Two miserable weeks out of the whole fifty-two! Two weeks—that was all you got for being caged up in a stuffy office with nothing but noise and traffic. Two weeks to do everything you wanted to, like going round the world, or living on a house-boat or in a gypsy camp, or alone in a tent a long way from everybody. At the end of the two weeks, back to the grind, getting there at the same time every morning and leaving at the same time every evening, and seeing the same frightful faces every day, like that girl at Roselle's office with a voice like a saw. That girl—and Roselle, shut up together all day long, taking orders from that gruesome man who ran the place. Roselle...who could have lived at home, if only she'd stood out against Lucille, if only she'd tried to keep them all together, if only she'd had any ideas of her own, instead of just that one idea of getting to London and having a career. If Roselle had only wanted to stay at home, perhaps something could have been done—something; anything. But with Lucille and Roselle both longing to leave, what chance had anybody of nine or ten? Nicholas could have done something if he'd been at home. Roselle could have done something, if only she'd been different— strong instead of sweet. But Roselle had put herself into a stuffy cage...

"Two weeks isn't long," said Belinda. "Why can't she go to Cornwall and stay with your sister Lucille?"

"Because Lucille..."   No! If she said she was getting

63

married, Belinda would go on and on to the very end, and the end...what was the end? Selling...she wouldn't say it, even to herself. Roselle wouldn't care and Lucille wouldn't care, and she didn't know about Nicholas, but Simon and Dominic—they'd feel as she was feeling. Or Simon would. At this moment, Simon would be feeling sick right down in the pit of his stomach, reading the letter...But what could Simon do? Who listened to them at their age? Nobody'd listen...but if they knew how she'd been feeling, if they knew that for the whole of the past year, she'd just been waiting, that was all, for the year to end, so's she could look forward to going home for the holidays—home, instead of...But if she had to do it for ever? Oh, please God, please God, please God, I know I only pray properly when I want something, but I swear, I swear I'll try and do something in return—if You'll just stop them from selling the house. Don't let Lucille sell our home, please God, please! Perhaps if You could make something happen to any of the people who want to buy it, whoever they are—if You could smite them, just so that there could be time to stop Lucille...please, God...

"What did you say?" Belinda's question brought Julia back with a sickening jolt.

"I didn't say anything."

"Yes, you did. You muttered something. Isn't it funny, I thought you said G-O-D."

"What would I say God for?"

"Hush! If Morley hears you, he'll think you're swearing.
64

"I might be praying."

"You wouldn't be praying in the middle of the afternoon like this—Oh Julia, you forgot to ask him to slow down at the Greenhurst crossroads."

"No. It doesn't matter."

She hadn't forgotten. She always leaned forward and tapped on the glass, and they went very slowly, slowly past the road that cut across this one and led...Well, she couldn't have borne it. Not to-day. And anyway, it was a long, long way. Even from here, it was a long way— and from Belinda's house, it was—well, it was miles and miles and miles. If she could stop the car now and get out— but she hadn't much money with her; not enough for a train fare. She could pay for a bus for part of the way. If she got as far as Penley's farm, she could make Doreen Penley lend her her bicycle. But if she was seen in her school coat and hat, so far from the school, people would notice...

She could borrow a coat and skirt from Belinda and hitch it up a bit here and there—then she could get home without attracting attention on the way. If she could get home to-night and stay with Lucille for just one night and come back the next day, Belinda's mother needn't tell the nuns anything. If she could only talk to Lucille...if she could only explain that home was a place where you kept your things and that your things were your life and that being parked with people for holidays, just with two suitcases, was the same thing as being cut in half and never being able to join up with your other piece. Up in the attic were all their treasures and it was no use Lucille saying "Tell me what you'd like to keep." If one hadn't wanted to keep them all, they wouldn't be up in the attic, would they, waiting until one could get at them again? Books...great, heavy books, hundreds of them. Whole sets of them. The whole *Swallow and Amazon* set; the whole *Doolittle* set; all the *Pollyannas*— the *Katy* ones and the *Little Women* ones; four different *Robinson Crusoes* and two *Wind in the Willows*; all the *Musketeers* and the 1936 Encyclopedias that Belinda's mother had turned out. The Violet Needhams and the Enid Blytons and all those old *Chatterboxes* that were found after Grandmother died, and the *Chums* that Mr. Milward had given Nicholas and Nicholas had passed on to her. Huge big books of Arthur and his Knights, and a book on horses and four volumes of Shakespeare, as new as on the day she got them, and three *Pilgrim's Progress*, all lovely and clean, and travel books and nursery books and holy books and adventure books. Who could carry them away from the attic and find room for them in Roselle's little room or in Aunt Mary's house, or in Lucille's new house, with that husband nobody knew anything about— and even if one could, where was there any place to read them? Where was the shrubbery and the great walled garden and the old clock-golf lawn and the overgrown tennis court? Where were the enormous trees, and the quiet places? And it wasn't only herself she was thinking of. She wasn't the only one who had treasures...There was the wonderful, the great, spacious, strong, livable-in tree house that Nicholas had helped them to build. It had rooms and a roof. It was Dominic's retreat. Dominic had worked and worked and worked and done his share in the making of it. And then...Long John. Oh, Simon, Simon, don't mind too much! I'll go and see Lucille, I swear I will, and I'll make her see...You can't go, Simon, but I can. I'll go; I'll make Lucille see that home is home and that people ought to have one...

"Belinda—"

"What?"

"Oh, nothing."

It was no use dragging Belinda into it. The less Belinda knew, the better. She, Julia, was going home and nobody was going to stop her. She was going to see Lucille. It was now—or never.

"Belinda, when we get to your house, may I borrow some clothes and wear them?"

"My goodness, you'd look funny! You're only half my size."

"I'm the same height—they'd just hang a bit, that's all. I'm tired of school clothes."

"I've got a new blue dress and jacket—you can wear that."

"No. Something sort of old."

They chose a grey suit, and Julia got into it. While Belinda was rolling on the floor in paroxysms of mirth at the figure she cut, Julia made her plans and was surprised at the ease and simplicity with which they fell into place. She had only to stay behind when Belinda and her mother drove out to fetch Belinda's father. She had only to slip out of the house when they had gone, and telephone back to the house and leave a message: Miss Julia Wayne had been summoned home by her sister and would return the following day.

The bus on the first part of the journey cost one and eightpence; that left her two and fourpence, which wasn't enough to get her to Penley's farm, but she could walk...And then, on Doreen's bicycle—why, on that she only had to pedal and then the miles would fly past and she would be home.

Home...and please, please God, do make Lucille listen...

Chapter Four

Roselle ruined the letter at once by bursting into tears and soaking it the moment she had read it through. Some of the lines were completely washed away; the remainder, though blotched, went on displaying their message all too clearly.

But there was no time to be spent in grieving; by the time she had cooked her breakfast egg on the gas ring and discovered that she couldn't swallow a mouthful of it, by the time she had repaired the damage done to her eyes by crying, it was a quarter to nine and she had to walk her fastest to get to the office.

Miss Stocker—thirtyish, fat, immovably placid and the firm's only other employee—glanced up from her deadly accurate typing, noted the tearstains and wondered, by no means for the first time, why people with nothing to cry about, did so much of it. Now, if *she*, she mused perplexedly, put her head down on her desk and howled like a tomcat, nobody could be surprised, for God knows, if ever a girl had something to cry about then she, Beryl Stocker, was the girl. But if she'd stopped to cry, she would have been drowned long ago—drowned in her tears—and nobody would have cared much. Life was what you made it, and she hadn't made it too badly, considering the start she'd had. She'd come all the way, unaided, from a council house in Greenwich right as far as Newbery's Travel Agency at Hyde Park Corner; it didn't look far to anybody else, perhaps, but she could remember the time when her clothes and her speech wouldn't have been correct enough to give her a job in a fish market, let alone here, right in the West End. She seldom tripped up over her grammar now—when she was taking care—and she could make the best of her clothes and her figure and her hair. Cry! 'Don't cry; try', her mother had said, and it was good advice, even if it was accompanied by a thump where it hurt most. Somebody ought to have told this Roselle Wayne that; look at her now, hanging up her coat and dropping tears all over it.

"Hey, stop that, young Roselle," requested Miss Stocker, not unkindly. "Tears don't melt troubles. What's gone wrong?" *'this time'*, she added, to herself.

Roselle glanced fearfully towards the door marked Private.

"He's not here," said Miss Stocker. "He was at the dogs last night, and if he backed what he said he was going to back, then he lost his pants. He'll come in looking as surly as surly and then we'll have to watch how we go. What's gone wrong?"

Roselle made no answer; she was wiping her eyes and taking a grip on herself with a resolution born of her fear of Mr. Newbery, her employer. He had a cautious habit of dictating half a dozen letters to each of his secretaries on the evening preceding one of his late appearances at the office; this relieved him of the searing anxiety of picturing them sitting at their desks next morning and doing nothing at his expense. If he came in before Roselle had finished her letters and laid them on his desk...Feeling as she did this morning, sarcasm from Mr. Newbery would be more than she could bear. She sat down, opened the incomprehensible series of squiggles she had put down at his dictation and stared at them hopelessly.

"Here—gimme," said Miss Stocker, holding out a hand.

Roselle, with a heart full of gratitude, handed over the book.

"You won't be able to understand it," she faltered.

"My!" Miss Stocker thumbed over the pages. "What speed did you get up to at that high-toned commercial school of yours?"

"I could do ninety," said Roselle, humbly.

Anybody could do ninety there, in the big, sunny classroom among girls like herself, all taking a pleasant and leisurely course that they were convinced would make them, in three or four months, the valued right hand of some dynamic but kind-hearted business executive. Anybody could do ninety in the comfortable hush of speed tests, the silence broken only by the twitter of birds in the gardens outside, or the steady, even tones of Miss Twyson, dictating with a stop watch in her hand. But who could get anything at all down when Mr. Newbery rapped out the words as though they were insults; when he made no secret of his contempt for her attainments, when he tore up as many of her letters as he signed? If it were not for Miss Stocker, who did all her own work with machine-like precision and then took over the bulk of Roselle's, Mr. Newbery would have dismissed her out of hand. It was a wonder he hadn't done so long ago.

It was no wonder to Miss Stocker, who, at fifteen, had been a handbook on human motives, and who now could read Mr. Newbery without effort. He kept her, B. Stocker, because she was drawing the pay of one and doing—efficiently—the work of two. Her place was at the typewriter; it was Roselle who had orders to receive clients and usher them into the presence. She, Beryl, was the stout, firm pedestal of the firm, and on the pedestal, Mr. Newbery placed the shy, pretty Roselle, whose gentle charm brought the Agency a type of client it had never before attracted. No other girl with Roselle's looks, Miss Stocker told herself grimly, as she inserted fresh paper into her machine, no girl with that roseleaf—roseleaf, huh! poetry!— beauty would have lasted a week once Mrs. Newbery—who paid frequent unheralded visits to the office, in order to see what Mr. Newbery was up to—caught sight of her. But nobody, not even Mrs. Newbery, could fail to be reassured by the clear, candid gaze of Roselle's blue eyes. Innocence! thought Miss Stocker, pounding the keys furiously. Innocence! in this day and age. Brought up by nuns, who taught her this meek-and-mild routine: be gentle, my daughter, be kind, my daughter; be good, my daughter. And then what? She came out into a wild wood, just like the fat-headed kid in the fairy story, who didn't know her own grandmother when she didn't see her—she came out with her soft little fingers all ready to hit the keys, and fell into this Newbery's calloused paws, and learned that busy men don't say Please and Thank You, and stand up when you come in, and run to help you off with your coat. Poor little kid, saddled with a lot of washed-up rules, and afraid to go out at night and enjoy herself, because all the boys in this wicked town wanted to end the evening up the cosy way. She, B. Stocker, had her own way of dealing with these hopeful Hotspurs, and some of them bore the scars to this day—but Roselle? She hadn't got it in her, and so she had stayed at home and missed a lot of fun.

"There." Miss Stocker finished five of Roselle's six letters and carried them over to her desk. "There you are. I won't do the last one; you wait till you hear him coming out of the lift, and then pretend you couldn't quite get through them. He'll smell a rat if you're ready with the lot. He'll—my! You're not crying again, are you?"

"Y-You're so kind," sobbed Roselle. "If it hadn't— hadn't been for y-you, I couldn't have b-borne it!"

The sobs which followed this acknowledgement were so bitter that Miss Stocker sat on the edge of her desk and regarded her colleague with a puzzled frown.

"Look, Roselle," she said slowly, "what I can't make out is why—if you hate it all so much—why you ever came to London!"

Roselle raised a countenance upon which disillusionment,

regret, and fear were equally visible.

"I didn't know it would be like this!" she said. "I thought—"

She walked to the window to recover herself, and stared down at the traffic swirling round Hyde Park Corner. Here she had stood a year ago, on her first day in the office, and had felt an uprush of excitement and joyous anticipation. London...at her feet. Well, there it was, still at her feet. There were the same cars, the same red buses, the same blue-clad policeman; there were the Park gates, and coming out of the Park were people like herself—nice-looking people, people who looked well brought-up, people she was used to meeting in Greenhurst. All she had wanted was to become one of a quiet, happy circle; a circle in which there might be, perhaps, some young men who would take her out sometimes to dinner, to a dance. Things went on in London—lots of things. You read about them in The *Tatler* and the *Sketch*; people went out and enjoyed themselves, evening after evening, and wore nice dresses like the ones she'd brought with her from home; girls went out—you saw their photographs in the papers, and however much you tried to be charitable, you couldn't help wondering what their escorts saw in them. All you wanted...all you had wanted was a good job, and some fun when the job was done for the day.

But the good jobs had demanded good qualifications, and she found that there were thousands—millions—of girls who could do what she did, and do it twice as well. Some of them, not content with being wonderful typists, could even speak languages and add up figures. And she couldn't help knowing that she was pretty but she had learned that there were also thousands—millions—of girls just as pretty...prettier. If she herself found men what the nuns had called bold, if she refused to go out with them, there were plenty of other girls who could have fun and still keep them in their place. But she couldn't...and she didn't want to, any more. And she hadn't known before she came to London, how noisy a big city could be; now it was a buzz and tangle in her head, day and night. There was no peace, no space, no time, no kindness, no understanding of lonely, green girls who came from the country. If she had been able to get home—out of London—at weekends, things might have been better. Sometimes she had thought, lately, of going down and staying with the Milwards at Greenhurst, but they—they and everybody else in Greenhurst—thought she was a successful business girl in London, and she wouldn't have been able to pretend. And now...since Lucille's letter had come this morning, she knew fully, for the first time, how much she had missed home, and how much she regretted ever leaving it.

Home! Was she to live for ever and ever in that drab cheerless room? Even that was more than she could afford. Money... her salary, by home standards, had sounded fabulous, but living here had melted it away. It came in a little envelope every Friday morning, and it ran away, flew away, melted away by Tuesday morning, and left her with nothing. If she lost this job and couldn't get another...and there was no home to fly to...no big rambling rooms, no comfortable dining room opening on to the lawn, no drawing room with the rose garden outside, no study, no library with the view of the big oak...Dominic's tree house...could Lucille really mean what she said about selling the house? She couldn't, she couldn't, she *couldn't*! This man she was marrying, whoever he was—he had never been home, had never seen it; if he had, he would have seen how lovely it was, he would have known that it was a house to—to hold on to—especially now, in June, with all the lovely colour in the garden. Wouldn't Lucille change her mind, and couldn't they all settle down there instead of in Cornwall? Lucille and her husband could live in one part of the house and she, Roselle could stay in the other part and keep house for Nicholas, and Simon and Julia and Dominic. Long John could come back from Mr. Hewett's and live with them again, and Julia could bring her books down from the attic and Dominic would be able to stay for long, long days up in his tree house. She wouldn't mind how hard she worked. She hadn't liked house-work much before, because she had preferred to think of herself as a business girl—but now! Oh, anybody could have that dreary room and this dreary, dreary job and this cruel, terrible city. All she wanted was to go home and never never leave it again. And Jeff was there....Jeff, who had loved her....

"Don't cry, poppet," came Miss Stocker's comforting voice. "Talk; it'll do you good. A pretty girl like you, weren't there any bright sparks down in your district that besought thee to stay there?"

"No. Well, yes," faltered Roselle. "There was one."

"Well, perhaps he looks more of a proposition now than he did a year ago," said Miss Stocker, sagely. "I don't know who had charge of you, but someone should have told you long ago that your type isn't made for rough wear. When I look at you, even I—me, B. Stocker!—even I think of outlandish things like lavender walks and China tea with lemon. I never saw anybody like you thrown to the lions before, and it worries me. What's more, it damps down that bit of fire my mum used to try and keep going inside me—believing in Providence, she called it. Who'd believe in a Providence that pulled you out of your little rose-bed and planted you right in the path of a laid-up battleship like Newbery? Why don't you take my advice, Roselle, and pop off back to where you came from?"

"I c-can't. My sister wrote...I got a letter from her this morning to say she's going to—to get married."

"Married? Who's she marrying?" enquired Miss Stocker.

"Someone I don't know."

"Well, sisters do get married, you know. It's bound to come later if it doesn't come now."

"It-it isn't that. She says she's going to live in Cornwall and s-sell the house."

"Sell the house? Your house?"

"Yes."

"The one down in where-was-it—Greenhurst?"

77

"Yes. She's made up her mind, and it's all practically s-settled. The people who were tenants have gone away and Lucille says she's put the house up for sale."

"Why all this Lucille-says and Lucille-does?" asked Miss Stocker, with a touch of irritation. "Does she have the only say-so?"

"Well, yes. You see, she's the—the sort of head of the family. My father died a long time ago and my mother was ill for a long time and anyway, she wasn't—she wasn't very good at managing things. She was—she was very nice, but she wasn't any good at business. Ever since my father died, Lucille's had to see to everything—even things like money, and choosing schools, all the things that parents usually do. She always arranged everything, even before my mother became ill. Then, when mother died, her money went to her sister and we didn't have enough to keep on the house, and so we...we let it. Lucille wanted to travel and I wanted to come to London and work here— it seems incredible now, but I didn't say anything to—to stop Lucille from sending Simon and Dominic to stay with an aunt, and I didn't—" Roselle's voice quavered—"I didn't even offer to stay on and try and manage somehow... When I look back, I think I must have been under a s-sort of evil spell. I didn't think of the children; I only thought about myself and about what I wanted to...what I thought I wanted to do. If I'd tried to make Lucille keep on the house, just to—to try and see if we could manage, perhaps she would have listened.

"And perhaps she wouldn't," said Miss Stocker, judicially. "She sounds to me the bossy sort. This man she's marrying will have his hands full, I daresay. I wouldn't like to cross her, not from the sound of her."

"Oh, but Lucille isn't at all—"

"What made your family string out the way it does?" asked Miss Stocker with deep interest. "All sorts and sizes, you are. You often see one baby pop up right at the tail end of a family, but I can't say I ever knew of an assorted lot like yours. How did it happen? The war, I suppose—was your father away?"

"No...no, he wasn't. Everybody thinks we're rather scattered and far apart, but we...we rather like it."

"'Tisn't a cheap way to have a family," commented Miss Stocker. "You can't make the first one's clothes do for the up-and-comings. They all—what's the matter?"

"I thought I heard Mr. Newbery."

"Well, and what if you did?" asked Miss Stocker sturdily. "There's nothing to get worried about, you know. He can't eat you; he won't beat you, and he won't molest you because his wife's always got a strong pair of glasses trained on him. So what's all the anxiety? Don't let him think you're frightened of him; it only brings out the bully in people."

"But I *am* frightened of him! I—I hate the way he talks to me, and the way he—"

"All right, all right—don't get upset again, my popsie— Look Roselle, joking apart, why don't you stop trying to make a go of things here and go back and have a nice talk with that sister of yours and see if you can't get her to have another think about selling the house? Why don't you have a shot at—"

"Oh, Miss Stocker, I'd do anything, anything, *anything*!"

"But that's only *talking*—that's not *doing*."

"But if I gave up this job, I'd never get another. Mr. Newbery would tell people that I'm...I'm no good, wouldn't he?

"Weren't there any jobs going in that place—Greenhurst?" enquired Miss Stocker, who felt disinclined to dwell on the subject of Roselle's qualifications. "Wasn't there something you could've tried there?"

"I—I didn't want to stay in Greenhurst—I wanted to come to London. I thought I'd like it—but I don't. And I don't like offices."

"Then keep out of them, that's my advice. There's plenty of my sort to fill them. Why don't you go back home?"

"It's too late." Roselle's tone was one of sheer desolation. "It's too late. Lucille said she was going to be at home to-day, to see about everything—all the final details. I'd have to *go* at once."

"Well then, go at once," urged Miss Stocker.

"I c-can't. If I left here, I'd have to give a week's notice!"

"Who said so?"

"Mr. Newbery said so, when he engaged me."

"Well, that was only what they all tell you, but it doesn't mean anything—not a thing," said the experienced Miss

Stocker. "You wouldn't have to give any notice—not if you didn't take the money, that is."

"H-How do you mean?"

"Your pay. Your screw, your salary; your weekly dollop. If you didn't take it—if you threw it back right in his face, you could go straight away. That's what's called giving a week's salary in lieu of notice; nobody could say a word to you if you did that. You could—well, here he comes. Now look, don't go and get upset if he comes in looking like a thunderburst; I looked up all his dogs and not one of them so much as got a third."

Mr. Newbery entered the office and strode through to his sanctum without pausing to extend the courtesy of a morning greeting. His bell rang furiously a moment later and Miss Stocker rose to answer it, taking her notebook and walking past Roselle's desk without speaking, but with her eyes raised Heavenward and a thumb and forefinger holding her nose to indicate her opinion of her employer. She was back before long and Mr. Newbery followed her, walked to Roselle's desk and threw on to it her letters of the previous day.

"Those can be done again—with corrections," he said acidly. He went back to his room and banged the door behind him; a moment later, it opened again, and his large purple countenance appeared round it. A pair of small, angry eyes glared at the shrinking Roselle. "And if it's all the same to you, Miss Wayne," he snarled, "Fiji is NOT spelt with four e's."

The door crashed once more; Roselle's tears flowed

afresh. Miss Stocker, banging the keys of her typewriter with one hand, managed to put out the other and bestow a maternal pat upon her colleague's shoulder.

"Don't worry," she whispered. "He'll go straight to hell one day, just you wait and see."

She went on with her work, and some time later, Mr. Newbery came in and dropped an envelope on each of their desks, his expression indicating clearly that the contents were twice as much as either of them was worth.

Miss Stocker slipped her envelope into her handbag and then, chancing to glance up at Roselle, remained open-mouthed, watching her strange behaviour.

Roselle's soft lips had set into a firm line. She pushed a sheet of paper into her typewriter and typed two lines on it. Drawing it out with a jerk, she put it, and with it her pay envelope, into a larger envelope, and addressed the latter one to her employer. Rising, she dropped the package on to Miss Stocker's desk and then walked to the peg on which her coat hung.

She got to the door before her movements showed any sign of hesitation, and then, as she turned and seemed to pause, Miss Stocker came out of her trance and sprang into action. Without speaking a word, she managed, in urgent pantomime, to convey clearly that it was as well to get going while the going was good, that Roselle had all her good wishes, that she would like to see her again, some time, somewhere; that she, Beryl Stocker, would take care of Mr. Newbery and prevent him from following his late employee. She would prevent him, if necessary, by force; she would bang him over the head with her new green umbrella over there, and lay him as flat as a pancake right under that table there. Now was the time to go, and swiftly, and yes, the notice was quite all right and she'd re-type it, because lieu wasn't spelt with a w, but quick was the word and sharp the motion, and go on, go on, go on, before the old hippopotamus came out and saw the only real lady who'd ever worked or who would ever work for him disappearing right under his nose.

Roselle darted swiftly across the room to drop a light kiss on her friend's hard brown cheek. Then she was gone, and Miss Stocker was left staring at the door, an expression in her eyes which very few people ever saw and which only her dead mother could have identified.

Chapter Five

Nicholas read the letter once, and then a second time, and then tore it into small pieces and threw it contemptuously to the wind.

Good timing, he thought, and went on with his packing.

A fellow got out of the Army after his two-year term, and just as he was making for home, his sister said "Hold it; there's no home: we're selling." Well, she'd have to think again. A nice girl, Lucille, but uppish; and while, two years ago, even one year ago, he might have been regarded as too young to have a say in family affairs, he was now twenty-one, and he knew what he wanted—and what he wanted most of all, now, was a home. The tenants were out; good. He would see to it that nobody else got in. Except themselves that is. Newest fiction; The Return of the Waynes. Watch the bookstalls.

It took money to live at Wood Mount; Lucille was right as far as that went, but stuck in the Army, he had been in no position, hitherto, to talk about helping towards the upkeep of the place. Now he was out, and they could get a slate and pencil and dot down a few figures and see how they stood. Sell? Yes, if they had to—but not in a hurry like this; not out of hand like this. It was their home and they needed a home; if the worst came to the worst, they could let it again for a time, until he got on his feet and was bringing in a bit of money. Lucille could go off and marry this Digby Whatsit; Roselle would have to give up that silly little fourth-rate job in London and come home— and from what he'd seen last time he dropped in on her, she was ready for a change. Julia? He grinned; try and keep Julia away from Wood Mount. Simon and Dominic: they ought to have a chance to live at home; this last year with Aunt Mary hadn't, in his opinion, been a good move—and now that this baby had appeared out of the blue, his own bet was that they wished they hadn't been so quick about taking Simon and Dominic in.

Home. Well, it was no good wasting time conjecturing; the thing was to get hold of some form of transport and get going.

He shook his money out of his pocket, out of his notecase, out of his newly-acquired tobacco pouch. Total, sixty-seven pounds, eight shillings and the odd pence. He oughtn't to have bought that trumpet off that fellow— but it was a bargain, and he couldn't regret it. He took it out of its case and played a few passages. Lovely! Oh, lovely! No, he couldn't regret it.

Well, he ought to be able to pick up one of those broken-down little cars he'd been nosing round inspecting lately; if it held up long enough to get him home, he'd tinker it up and make it as good as new. He mightn't be a bright boy in lots of ways, but *(a)* he could play a trumpet, and *(b)* he knew an engine when he saw one. He'd go out to that fellow in Chiswick and see how much he'd knock off that little scarlet number...

Nicholas went to Chiswick and entered the vast garage in which, in a far corner, reposed the scarlet number. While he was looking at it, he was joined by a smooth-sounding salesman who introduced himself as Mr. Druce, entirely at his client's service. What could he—?

Nicholas emerged forty minutes later with eighteen shillings and some odd pence in his pocket, the owner of a motor-cycle and side-car. It was a long road from the scarlet two-seater to a motor-bike and side-car, but Mr. Druce had led him along it imperceptibly, irresistibly; it was not until the money had been counted out and checked in the Office that Nicholas remembered that even if he had wanted a motor-bike, he had no use, no liking and no desire for a side-car. But here it was; he'd got it.

He pushed the combination to the river and, leaning it against a tree, walked a few paces away and studied his new possession. A motor-bike and side-car—his! Fancy!

Well, it was transport. He wheeled it into the road, kicked it to life and started on his journey.

Hunger and thirst brought him to a halt at a roadhouse on the outskirts of London. Parking his seedy-looking vehicle between two glossy sports cars, he went into the crowded bar and ordered a beer. Drinking it slowly, he looked round at the assembled company and found that most of them formed one group around an exuberant gentleman called Joey. Nicholas listened to him with some enjoyment and learned that he was a professional photographer—freelance—whose work appeared in all the well-known magazines and who was on first-name terms with scores of celebrities. The talk was not all personal; in between anecdotes of famous men and women, Joey had a good deal to say about his work—and as he preferred to say it to as large an audience as possible, Nicholas found not only that his next beer was a free one donated by Joey, but also that he had become one more of Joey's innumerable friends. More, he was seated, half an hour later, at a table for two, in the large, sunny dining-room, with Joey—large, expansive, florid and cheerful—seated opposite.

A somewhat supercilious waiter approached with a menu, and Joey made short work of him.

"'Morning, Charlie; how's the gout?"

"I do not suffer from gout, sir."

"Then don't look as though you did. If you're healthy, smile—come on, boy—smile. He can't," he confided in an aside to Nicholas. "He's left it too long. Well, never mind, Charlie; let's see what's on the card to-day. This is on me, young feller." he told Nicholas.

"You're very kind," said Nicholas, with unanswerable firmness, "but I'm paying for my own lunch—and I'd like to buy you a beer in return for one you bought me, if you'll have one."

"The proud type," Joey told Charlie. "Haughty. Up-stage. Independent turn of mind. Well, thank God, I never turned down a good offer when anybody made me one; if some-body'd offered me a lunch when I was your age, young shaver, I'd have said yes, and quick. All right then, Charlie, separate bills. Trout for me," he decided, scanning the menu. "Nice bit of trout to start with, and then...lemme see...pork chops, I shouldn't wonder. Yes, that's it; a nice bit of fresh trout and then the pork chop, and I'll follow it up with a bit of Stilton. And I'll have that beer this young feller offered me, and you can put it on his bill." He handed the menu to Nicholas. "Now it's your turn."

Nicholas glanced down the price list and handed the menu to the waiter.

"Ham and salad," he said.

"Oh, come, come, *come!*" protested Joey. "You can have ham and salad at one of those snooty little cafes down the road run by bony gentlewomen. You can get *food* here—decent food. What's the matter? Low in the pocket?"

"Very," said Nicholas, with a smile. "Ham and salad, waiter."

"Oh, well—" Joey leaned back resignedly— "I'd like to give you a good lunch; I hate to see good food go to waste—but if you've decided to be poor but proud, then there's nothing more to be said. Ah—beer." He raised his tankard. "Here's to women, God bless 'em. My name's Helyon, spelt with a y and not with two l's; what's yours?"

"Nicholas Wayne."

"You looked a bit cold when you came in. Bad circulation?"

"No. Been on a motor bike. It's cold work."

Joey's eyes roved over him frankly.

"Just out of t'Army, I expect," he summed up.

"Yes."

"What're you going to do now?"

"I've no idea."

"What—no ambition?"

Nicholas laughed. "Plenty—but for the moment, I'm going home."

"Where's home, chum?"

"Hampshire. Place called Greenhurst—or near it. About four miles away. Do you know it?"

"Don't know Greenhurst, but I'm going there on a job in a day or two—taking a movie of a place for a client. I get a lot of this kind of job; a chap with a big property gets the idea that he'd like to have a film made of it—house, inside and out; grounds, lake and so on. This is a fellow called Lord Templeby—heard of him?"

"They live a mile and a half away from us."

"Well, well, well. Any beautiful daughters?"

"One. Not beautiful; passable."

"Good. Not that they're putting me up, mark you. I've got to find my own digs. What's the local pub called?"

"The George. It's quite good."

"Then it's the George for me. I'll give you a ring and we'll start the beer flowing again—yes?" Joey leaned back to allow the waiter to put his plate before him. "Ah—good smell that, Charlie. Where's my friend's ham and greenery?"

"Coming shortly, sir."

"Step on it, then." Joey picked up his fish knife and fork and began to eat with enjoyment. "It's good; it's really good," he told Nicholas. "You're missing a treat." He missed a good many other treats, reflected Nicholas, and for the same reason that he was missing this one: lack of funds. He looked with pleasurable anticipation at the plate of ham and salad the waiter set before him, and reached for the mustard. He was about to begin his meal when Joey leaned across the table and seized Nicholas's arm just as it was lifting the first mouthful to his lips.

"Ah-ah-ah-ah-ah," he said warningly. "Wait a minute, wait a minute." He turned in his chair and summoned the waiter peremptorily. "Hey—Charlie! Here a minute.

Look," he told him severely on his arrival, "This won't do, you know. This young chap didn't come in for a free meal; he's paying for what he gets, and no friend of mine's going to pay for a salad that looks as tired as that one. Look at it! Look at that lettuce! It's like you—sad. Drooping. Languid. Take it away, Charlie, and tell 'em to give it to the chickens. Tell 'em Joey said so. And then you just bring my friend here a salad—a real salad. Not a bit of tired lettuce and a tomato crescent and those imitation green rushes. Go on, take it back, Charlie, take it back, take it back."

The waiter, a picture of outrage, carried away the plate, and Nicholas looked across the table in some dismay.

"But it was—"

Joey put up a huge hand to demand silence.

"Now, you'd have eaten that, wouldn't you?"

"Yes."

"And that's where you go wrong, son," Joey told him earnestly. "That's where you let the side down. You take what they give you, and if they give you less than your money's worth, you're too impatient, or too nice, or too frightened or too plain damned lazy to make a fuss and throw it right back at 'em. And so what? The next feller gets the same treatment. If you're paying, Nicholas my boy, you're entitled to a bob's worth for every shilling you lay out. Not for your own sake— not only for your own sake, but to keep up the general level. Now here comes Charlie with what you're paying for—see? That's right, Charlie; put it down, put it down. Now *that's* a salad. In fact, Charlie, it looks so good, you can bring me another like it with the pork. Now you tuck into that, young man, and enjoy it—and next time, have a look to see what you're getting—and don't be afraid to make a hell of a fuss if you're not being treated right."

Nicholas ate with relish and gratitude; Joey put away pork, potatoes, vegetables, salad and then followed these with a generous helping of cheese. Leaning back at last replete, contented, he looked across at Nicholas with his broad face gleaming with friendliness.

"Feel a lot better," he confided. "I'm a warm man and I need a lot of stoking. How're you getting down to Greenhurst? Oh, yes, I forgot—your bike."

"Yes. If you'd care for a lift, I'd be—"

"Outside," Joey told him, "you'll see a big yellow convertible. Mine. It's a showy piece, but I have to have a good car in my job: I get some of these top-line actresses sometimes to come out and stand about decorating a place I'm photographing, and I have to give 'em transport of the kind they'd like you to think they were accustomed to. Shop window. Don't you ever begrudge money laid out on your shop window, son; it pays hands down. My old dad taught me that—among other things. My word, what a grand old boy! Twelve kids—I was number eleven—and all we had to start us out in life was the old man's advice. Bit of a philosopher he was; used to say that all that kids needed to be taught was how to rough it and how to be happy on nothing. Simple, but by God, it worked with the whole round dozen of us. Half the youngsters they turn out nowadays waste good years before they find their own level—like you, for example. That waiter chap takes one look at you and knows you'd eat the sort of salad I'd send away. It ought to be the other way round, because you're a fine young type with good upbringing sticking out all over you, and I'm... well, I'm not. But they haven't taught you how to get value, and that hurts me because I like you." Joey broke off to study the bill the waiter brought and laid a note on the plate. "Now look," he said, "when it comes to your turn to tip, you make it ten per cent, instead of twelve per cent., see? That'll drive home the point to Charlie. Next time you come in here, you'll get service."

He followed Nicholas out into the road and seemed reluctant to part from him.

"Look out for me in Greenhurst," he said. "I'll turn up one day. Then you..." He stopped and stared. "That's not your bike, is it?"

"Well—yes; as a matter of fact, it is."

"Oh! You've knocked her about a bit, haven't you?"

"Not really. I only bought it this morning."

"You only *what*?"

"I only—"

"I don't believe it. Nobody could sell anybody a bike in that condition."

"It isn't bad; I mean it's—"

"Boy," intoned Joey, sadly, "have you been cooked!"

"It goes all right," said Nicholas, mutinously.

"What did they screw out of you for that bit of scrap?" Nicholas told him and Joey stared at him, speechless. Recovering at last, he spoke impulsively. "Look here, now," he said. "Look, let's you and me go back to those highway robbers you bought it from. Just let me talk to them. I'll have your money out of their coffers and back in your pocket before you can—"

"No," Nicholas spoke firmly. "No. You're very kind, Mr. Helyon, and I'm very grateful to you and I'll try to take your advice in future, but I bought the bike and if I'm a mug, then I'm a mug."

"You certainly are that," agreed Joey sadly. "Well then, go ahead and ride it as long as it holds together—and I hope your teeth don't rattle right out of their sockets. Well, so long, and thanks for the beer."

He shook hands with Nicholas and walked to the large, loud car standing a few yards away. Nicholas looked after him with regret; he had been good company, this Joey, and he was sorry to see him go.

Ships that pass, he reflected, straddling his bike.

He left the town behind him, and for a time, was occupied in listening to the squeaks and groans and howls proceeding from various parts of the machine. Then he forgot them and remembered only that he was on his way home; already there were one or two familiar landmarks; he was nearly there.

Home—and Lucille would have to listen to him. She might be the eldest, but he was the man of the family and from now on, he was going to have a say in their affairs.

He began to sing; then he gave out a loud and extremely good imitation of a trumpet and performed a rhythmic *obligato* to the background of sound coming from his motor-bike. His spirits lifted, his speed increased. *Where-ever we may*

wander, poo-poo, poo-too-too-poo, there's no ho per-lace like
hoooome...

Home. He had no wife, he had no girl, he had no job.
All he had in the world was a silver-toned trumpet and a rat-
tle-shake motor-bike. And a side-car. But that was enough for
the present. The other things would come. Things came, in
time. Lucille hadn't learned that; here she was, still on the
rush; rushing into marriage, rushing away from a beautiful
home like Wood Mount.

Home. *Phoo-poo-poo-phoo doddly poo poo poo.* What a
passage! He must try that over as soon as he could get home
and get at his trumpet. Music.

Music—and home.

Chapter Six

From Shrewsbury, the journey had been uneventful; there had, that is to say, been no alarm, no pursuit and—deepest relief of all to Simon—not the least indication that their fellow-passengers regarded them as anything but two boys going upon their lawful ways. There was nothing to be worried about; nevertheless, when the train drew into the station in London, Simon found that the journey with Dominic had been an exhausting experience.

There was nothing, outwardly, to account for this. Dominic was quiet, even docile; he seldom left his seat in order to wander up and down the corridors; he answered remarks from strangers with studious politeness, and he read the book Simon had bought for him to read. But he had a way of becoming engrossed in incidents which Simon, busy with the details of tickets and timings and platform numbers, missed altogether; thus, one moment, Dominic would be walking beside him and the next, his remarks would be addressed to empty air or to surprised strangers. Each time this happened, Simon would have to stop, turn, and make his way back to the point at which Dominic still stood, gazing at something that had attracted his attention: the faulty lock in the train lavatory that would be sure to trap the next person going in—and did; the porter with the heavy barrow, who wouldn't be able to stop before bumping into the woman with the feather—and couldn't. He always had to wait and see the result of his calculations; this invariably took time, and when Simon at last lost his temper, after hours of untiring patience, and jerked him by the arm, it was to find, as he always found when this happened, that people thought he was ill-treating Dominic. When he had hauled Dominic back to stop him from getting off the train before it had quite stopped, an elderly woman nearby had given an indignant croak and taken a firmer grip on her umbrella. A porter on the platform gave Simon a terrible look and hissed "Nah then, 'ands orf 'im, the pore little thing." Dominic's appearance was very misleading—or perhaps, thought Simon, his own was. He had heard people say, sometimes, that Dominic looked like an angel—it was no wonder that strangers were misled into imagining that he was as good as he looked.

It was a shock to discover when they had crossed London that they were just in time to meet, head-on, the rush of workers leaving the city and bound for week-ends in the country. They stepped from their bus in the station yard straight into a seething, struggling mass of humanity and Simon, keeping a desperate hold on Dominic, fought and battled against the tide that threatened to sweep them on to the wrong platform. The small case he carried was torn from his grasp; with it went their tea and two suits of pyjamas. His mackintosh belt was ripped off and in an agonising moment, he lost his grip on his brother.

When the crowd had at last surged past them and the train, packed to capacity, had drawn away, they were left to assess the damage and to retrieve the case. They found it, trodden to a pulp; the sandwiches were a total loss, but the pyjamas would be all right, thought Simon, when they had the mud scraped off them. The food didn't matter much; Dominic had eaten well on the journey, because people always gave him a share of whatever they happened to have with them; he had got through several different kinds of sandwiches, innumerable buns and a good deal of chocolate. Dominic never felt in the least sick on a train, whereas he, Simon, spent the whole journey fighting off nausea....

Now they must find the platform from which the Greenhurst train would leave; Simon hoped with all his heart that it wouldn't be as crowded as the train that had just left the station.

When they found the right platform, however, he saw that if they got through the crowds and on to the train at all, it would be a miracle. Hundreds, thousands of people it seemed to him, were jostling, struggling, fighting their way on.

He grasped Dominic's arm firmly.

"Look," he said, "you stay close to me and when I say push, you push, and...and p'raps we'll get on to the train."

They made little headway, but suddenly there was an easing—a parting of the crowd in front of them, and Simon pushed Dominic into the opening. The next moment, the crowd had closed inexorably and he found that Dominic had been jerked from his clasp and was being taken slowly but irresistibly towards the train, while he himself was being forced back and back; the gap between them widened, and with a sick feeling of disaster, he realised that he had lost sight of Dominic...Dominic was lost in that cruel mass of humanity...Dominic...

And then he saw him. He was being borne by the pressure of the crowd to the door of a carriage. He was in the train. He vanished again and then his face—anxious, searching, appeared at a window. Simon tried to signal, but he was being pushed to the edge of the crowd. Now he was free of it, no longer being squeezed, suffocated—but he was hopelessly separated from Dominic. Behind him was a wide clear space, with only a few people walking from a train which had just pulled in and which, obviously, was not going out again for some time, as no crowds were milling towards it. In front of him were more and more people—and Dominic was on the train and he couldn't get through to him—and perhaps he would be frightened and try to get out and...

Dizzy with fear, Simon moved backwards in the hope of isolating himself from the crowd and becoming visible to his brother. If Dominic could see him—if he could signal to him to go on, if he could make him understand that he would come on the next train...

But he was too small...He couldn't see over all those

heads. He shouldn't have come; he shouldn't have left Aunt Mary's and come on this terrible, this ill-fated journey. He had been responsible for Dominic, and he had failed him.

A great sob shook Simon. Straining on tip-toe, craning his neck, he wept openly, and a man passing on his way to the exit stopped to look at him. After a moment, he came up to put a hand on Simon's shoulder.

"What's the matter?"

Simon glanced up. He was a tall, broad man—a man who gave the impression of strength and dependability, a man with firm lips and kind eyes, and a sympathetic look. He dashed the tears from his eyes and spoke hurriedly. "It's Dominic—it's my brother. We—we got separated and he's littler than me and I was in charge of him and—"

"Where is he?"

"He got on the train—he's there, but he can't see me, and he'll go in a minute and..."

"Half a moment." The man put down a suitcase, lifted Simon and swung him with greatest of ease on to his shoulder.

"Now," he said, "show me."

"There—oh, there! Dominic, Dominic!"

Simon, from his magnificent grandstand, waved frantically; from the window, Dominic saw him and raised a hand in response.

"He's seen me! He's seen me! Look, he's waving!"

"Now, listen," said Simon's new friend, "signal to him to

go on."

"To-"

"Yes; to go on. Make him understand that you'll follow."

"Oh—yes!"

He pointed in the direction—he hoped—of Greenhurst, and he saw Dominic nod. As best he could, Simon mimed the information that he would follow as soon as possible. Again Dominic nodded and smiled—and then the train drew out and took him away—alone.

The man lifted Simon down and stood looking at him. "Well, there you are," he said. "All you needed was a bit more height. Where were you bound for?"

"Greenhurst."

"That's in Hampshire, isn't it?"

"Yes. Thank you for helping me," said Simon. "I'll wait for the next train and perhaps it won't be so crowded." The man studied the small, white, tired face.

"Have you come far," he asked.

"We came from near Shrewsbury—first we took a bus and then we got a train. We—we're going home because..." a tear forced its way out and Simon ignored it "—because we—we wanted to. But we didn't ask if we could come."

"That doesn't sound very sensible. Didn't ask whom?"

"My uncle and aunt. We live with them, but my sister was going to sell our house in Greenhurst and we—we came to tell her not to."

It was a relief to tell someone—someone who looked so reliable.

"My name's Debrett—Robert Debrett." He paused imperceptibly, as though expecting Simon to recognise it, but Simon gave no sign. "What's yours?"

"Simon Meredith Wayne. I'm eleven and Dominic's nine."

"Well, Simon, how about some tea?"

Simon shook his head.

"No, thank you very much," he said politely. "I feel rather sick in trains and so I don't like to eat much." He shifted his case and held out a small, grimy hand. "Good-bye, sir, and thank you very much."

"Hold on now." Robert Debrett hesitated for a few seconds to examine the impulse, and then decided to give way to it. "There's no need to go on by train. I've got my car here; I'll run you down to Greenhurst."

"Oh..." A flush of relief, of hope, crept into Simon's cheeks, and the look in his eyes made Robert Debrett ashamed of the few seconds' hesitation. "Could...I mean, if you're really going that way—"

"I am," said Robert, who had been going to his flat in Knightsbridge. "But as we're driving, suppose we have some tea first—or I tell you what, we'll get out of town first and then choose a nice place in the open—how's that?"

This wasn't, thought Simon, studying him gratefully, like

talking to strangers, a thing he had been warned against. This was no stranger; this was a man who had understood at once that Dominic was being carried off alone; this was a man nobody could call anything but good and kind.

"We'll go to Greenhurst and pick Dominic up at the station," said Robert, answering the scrutiny. "Then I'll drive you home and we'll explain to your parents how we got together— yes?"

"I haven't any parents, but—"

"Well, I'll explain to your sister. Let's get going."

Simon found himself walking beside his new-found friend and accompanying him to the station exit. A chauffeur standing by a beautiful car came up, saluted, and took the suitcase, and Robert Debrett opened the front door of the car.

"In you go, young Simon," he said, and helped him up into the seat beside the driver's. Then he spoke in a low voice to his chauffeur.

"I shan't need you, Langley; and tell them not to wait up for me; I'll probably be late. You might find a place called Greenhurst for me, will you?"

They bent their heads over a map and then Robert gave another low direction to the man before getting in beside Simon.

"Nobody's to know where I am," he instructed him.

"Very good, sir."

"Can we race the train?" inquired Simon, as the car slid

out of the line of lesser vehicles and gathered speed.

"If we want to—but we'll try to make it a dead heat— with a stop for tea as our handicap. Why don't you lean back and make yourself comfortable? We've got a long journey ahead."

"How long will it take?"

"What time was the train due at Greenhurst?"

"Six ten."

"Then it'll take us until six ten."

"This is a Rolls, isn't it?"

"Yes."

"I knew by that thing on the front. Nicholas taught us about cars."

"Nicholas?"

"He's my brother. He's been in the Army, but I think he's out now."

"A sister and a brother—and Dominic."

"And Roselle—and Julia."

"Quite a family. Who's in charge?—the uncle and aunt?"

"Oh no! Lucille's the—the head of the family. But Lucille's going to get married and she wrote and said she wanted to sell the house, but our things are in it and..." Robert Debrett stole a glance at his young companion and then settled down in his seat to listen. A smile appeared on his lips, and a gleam of amusement and interest in his eyes.

"Yes? Your things are in it, and so—?"

Simon proceeded to tell him.

Chapter Seven

The walk to Penley's farm seemed endless. The road went on, and on, and on. It was a hot road, a dusty road. Of the original two and fourpence, eightpence had gone on a milk shake in Lowdale; that left one and eightpence; Julia counted it for the third time. She would be able to buy something to eat at Penley's...if she ever got to Penley's. How many more miles? If only she had her gym shoes on...but these were her best strap shoes with the thin soles—at least, the soles had been thin, but now they had worn practically away. Oh, for a bicycle! A bicycle! Once on Doreen Penley's bicycle, she would be able to put the miles behind her—so easily, so effortlessly.

There was a bit of poetry—she didn't like poetry much, but she couldn't help thinking of that now, something about a road:

> 'Does the road wind uphill all the way?
> Yes, to the very end'.

Well, this one certainly seemed to.

Hot! If it was hotter than this in the Sahara, then she was sorry for the Saharians, that's all; they could have it, camels and *oasises* and all, she told herself.

Was that Lapwing Hall? Oh good, oh good, oh good! Only another two miles to Penley's...and then Doreen's bicycle.

But when Julia reached Penley's farm, it was to learn that Doreen Penley was away from home...and she had taken her bicycle with her.

The news was shattering. Julia received it over the glass of milk she had bought; she put the glass down slowly and tried to understand what this blow would mean.

She saw Mrs. Penley looking at her curiously, and fought to appear unconcerned. Doreen was a friend, but Mrs. Penley—she wasn't exactly an enemy, Julia reflected, but she was by no means an ally, as Doreen would have been. If she got suspicious...if she rang up the school....

"What are you doing out of school?" inquired Mrs. Penley, sitting down opposite to Julia at the kitchen table and looking at her searchingly.

"My sister's thinking of selling our house, and we've got to go there and decide which of our things we'll keep and which will be sold," said Julia, with every appearance of ingenuousness.

There was nothing like the truth for convincing people, she thought. Mrs. Penley looked quite different; she'd been prepared for a lot of yarns, but she'd known all the time about the house being sold.

"Why didn't you go home by train?"

"I wasn't at school; I was staying with my friend Belinda, it wasn't until I got on the bus to go to Lowdale that I saw I hadn't got enough money with me—so I thought I could come here and do the rest of the journey on Doreen's bike and send it back to-morrow by the carrier."

"Well, she's not here, as I told you. You can't walk all that way; you'd better wait for Mr. Penley to finish in the hayfield and he'll run you back in the car."

"Thank you, but I'm not a bit tired," said Julia.

If she waited, she knew with certainty that Mrs. Penley would do some telephoning. She had to get away...at once. It was a dreadful, a bitter disappointment, but if she didn't get away...they'd start telephoning—to the school, to Lucille...She must get away.

She rose and put down her empty glass.

"That was nice, thank you," she said.

"Would you like a bit of cake to take with you?"

Julia would have given her soul for a piece of cake, but to appear hungry would arouse suspicion.

"No, thank you," she said. "Good bye, Mrs. Penley."

"Good-bye. I'm sorry Doreen wasn't here."

"It doesn't matter. Good-bye."

She went out into the yard and through the big farm gates. She heard the kitchen door close behind her, and then, with a swift rush, she doubled back and went into the feed store. She had remembered that Doreen's wasn't the only bicycle on the farm—she had seen another lying in a corner of the feed store—whose, she had no idea, but it had looked abandoned. It was probably an old one of Mr. Penley's. Yes—it was there, in the corner.

Julia walked over and examined it. It was old and rusty and in deplorable condition—but it had wheels, she noted with deep thankfulness; the tyres looked worn out, but she didn't care—there were two wheels, and she could pedal her way home and rest her aching feet. She would send the bike back to-morrow—and ten to one they'd never notice it had gone.

She wheeled the machine outside and looked cautiously down the road. There was nobody about; she heard voices from the hayfield and knew that every available man, woman and child would be working there, forking hay as long as the light lasted. She was safe from observation.

She gave the bike a preliminary push, hopping along with one foot on the pedal. The tyres were flat, but there was no pump and in any case she could not stop to use it. The bike was too large; swinging a leg over the bar and settling herself on the saddle, she found that to pedal at all she must shift her hips from side to side on the saddle; at this rate, she thought grimly, she would get home skinless—but for the moment, she was off her feet; she was moving—really moving, and not just plodding. The road was flying past her—or so it seemed, after her recent snail's progress.

She looked ahead, her mind measuring the distance between here and home. It was uncomfortable riding, and the road surface, she knew from experience, didn't get any better. Steering a too-large bike like this was difficult— but she only had to stay on and keep pedalling...pedalling...pedalling, and she would get home in time. It was hot work; it was gruelling work; but she had only to keep on and she would get there. Home. Nine, perhaps ten miles—it was nothing. Lots of people had been hungrier than this, tireder than this, hotter than this—and they had kept on. She would keep on...pedalling, pedalling...pedalling. The road was long and it was bumpy, but it was quiet and she was not likely to meet anybody; there were no farms, no houses along the route, and she had often ridden this way in the past without meeting a soul. Nobody would see her; she was safe from observation, from pursuit. The road was hers.

The road was not quite hers. Some miles ahead, plodding as Julia had lately plodded, went a gentleman called Pietro Faccini.

Signor Faccini was on his way to America. This was, perhaps, not a direct route, but Pietro, with the unquenchable optimism which had kept him smiling for all his thirty-one years of life, had no doubt at all that he would, in time, reach Greenwich Village, New York City. His. brother, Giuseppi, had sent him the fare—all the way from New York to the village of Constanzia, near Genoa; all Pietro had to do, said Giuseppi, was to take the boat from Genoa to New York; there he would be met and given a job, given a home, given money.

It had been an alluring prospect, and Pietro had given his notice at once to the restaurant proprietor at Constanzia. It was the beginning of the tourist season and the proprietor had not wanted to lose his waiter, washer-up and assistant cook, but Pietro had not heard his protests, having by that time begun his journey.

But he had not gone to Genoa. He had seen Genoa many times; now that he had journey money, he would make the journey an interesting one; he would not merely go to Genoa and get on a boat and see nothing but ocean; he would join his brother by a longer, a better, a more interesting route. He would see other places on the way— France, Switzerland, England; from England, he would get a boat that would take him to New York, and by then he would have become a much-travelled man of the world; a cosmopolitan, a man who would be able to discourse—and how well he discoursed it was not for him to say—upon the capitals of Europe; who could speak of Paris and London with first-hand knowledge. To Genoa and then on to a boat? It was unthinkable. One must spin out this thing.

The trip had spun out, but the money, unfortunately, had run out. Pietro cooked in Switzerland, waited at restaurant tables in Paris and washed up in London. Now he was on his way to Southampton—but still by a somewhat circuitous route, for before he could board a ship, it was necessary to have passage money; to earn this, he had taken a job with the Venetian Brush Company—and he was marching along the highway in order to save his train fare, and he was presenting himself at front doors and taking off his new English hat and fishing in his new English waistcoat pocket for his firm's card and presenting it with a flourish, before discoursing on the subject of brushes.

He had not fully understood, he thought, as he walked along the long, dusty road, how fine a gift of salesmanship he possessed. It might be the new clothes he wore that gave him confidence—he could not say. Not that they were new clothes; they were second or third or fourth hand, and they did not fit him; they were too big here, too small there—but they were all of a piece; there was the elegantly striped jacket and waistcoat and the striped trousers of the same pattern; his shoes were not of the same high standard, being of canvas—not clean and not even whole, but a man could not have everything—and the trousers were fortunately long enough to hide them. It had been necessary, the manager had said, to rig himself out before taking up his salesman's post. Fully rigged, he had presented himself and they had given him the little case full of brushes. "There's one thing," the manager had said, "when they see you standing there, they won't shut the door—not at once"—and he had looked wonderingly at Pietro's new hat and, below it, the dark-skinned, somewhat long face, the noble nose, the luxuriant black curling hair and the large, liquid brown eyes.

A salesman. It was a pity, browsed Pietro, that he could not sell on the spot; having worked the housewife up into a state in which she would have bought all his wares, suitcase and all, it was humiliating—it was an anti-climax to have to pack his samples away again, take her name and address and merely promise her brushes in the future. He would have liked to have a car, a van, a pantechnicon full of brushes, one for every room in every house at which he called. It was a pity he had spent his...Giuseppi's capital. He could have set himself up in brushes and made his fortune here in England, and gone to America a rich man instead of a humble younger brother.

It was hot! It was a pity he had had no money to spare for a cool drink. An ice! How wonderful the feeling of an ice-cream would be, trickling down his parched throat. Even water would do—but the only liquid in sight was the dark brown, murky ooze in the ditch running beside the road.

Pietro's imagination, which seemed always to work most cheerfully in adversity, here came to relieve his distress; for the next mile or so, he walked in a happy dream in which a large car drove silently by and stopped some way ahead; from one of its windows appeared a white, rounded arm; answering its invitation, he hurried along and found himself looking into the car, into a pair of glowing eyes. A uniformed lackey opened the door; Pietro stepped in and was borne along a wide, tree-shadowed avenue beside his beautiful companion. Pressing a secret spring, she opened a cabinet and disclosed two glasses and a tall, slender-necked bottle; he opened it and they drank, and the wine was cool, cool as her lips were warm. She took his glass from him and her lovely arms closed round him. Drawing him to her, she—

At this interesting point, Pietro stumbled on a large stone and had to stop to recover his hat. When he had picked it up and put it back on his head, the lovely woman and the car had vanished, and he was alone on the dusty road once more.

And yet not quite alone. Glancing back over his shoulder he saw that behind him, in the distance, was a bicycle. He gave it no more than a glance, and then walked on; this was no gleaming car, and there was no lovely woman—only a little boy, or a little girl on a machine that looked to be too big and that wobbled dangerously from one side of the road to the other.

Remembering this fact, Pietro moved himself cautiously to the extreme edge of the road; he had no wish to find his new suit brushed by dusty bicycle wheels.

Behind him, Julia came on. She was riding, by now, in a dream—but not of the delightful kind that whiled away the minutes and the miles for Pietro. She had fallen off twice, and her clothes were torn and dishevelled. Her hat was gone, her elbows were showing through her sleeves, her face was tear-stained and mud-streaked and there was a buzzing in her ears. She had very little idea where she was—but this was the road and she had to keep on it. Somewhere along it was home. She would come to it in time...perhaps.

She saw a figure ahead, and then it became two figures, both dim, both hazy. She tightened her grip on the handlebars, but she was on a bicycle that had proved, more than once, to have ideas of its own. She steered for a point midway between the two figures, and plunged on.

The next moment, something hit Pietro straight between the shoulders and sent him flying. His suitcase went one way, his hat another; Pietro himself went straight into the ditch, and on top of him came a large bicycle.

"Mother of God," he said in his own language. "Am I a cow that I should be—"

He stopped. Wet, filthy, dripping clods of mud, he stared over the side of the ditch into a pair of frightened, streaming eyes.

"Oh!" cried Julia, "Oh, are you...are you hurt?"

Pietro said nothing, for suddenly his heart was too full for speech. He could only gaze at her, this thin little girl with the red stringy hair and the dirty face and the torn clothes—-this little girl on this huge bicycle which had plunged him into the ditch—this exhausted-looking, this dreary little miss, who—herself scratched, bleeding—could yet look at him and, forgetting herself and her troubles, cry out in concern for him, Pietro Faccini—could ask if he was hurt.

He scrambled out and held out a muddy hand to help her up.

"Me? Hurt? How can a toss into a ditch hurt me, a so-big fellow?" he asked in magnificent astonishment. "All that is for me is a little mud, yes? And I say to myself, how lucky for me that I had my bad clothes—that will not be spoilt. A hot sun to dry them, and then a brush—see, I have a whole box full of brushes."

There was not quite a boxful; the suitcase had burst open, and a good proportion of Pietro's stock-in-trade lay in the ditch.

"Oh," said Julia, "you were selling brushes and they're...I've spoiled them!"

"You? No, no, no!" protested Pietro. "And nothing is spoiled—nothing. Now let me look and see if you have hurt your arm."

"It's nothing," said Julia, surveying a number of scratches and bruises. "That was the last time I fell off."

"You fell off before?"

"Yes, twice. The bike's too big, and I shouldn't have ridden it when the tyres were flat, and the road was bad and they came off in the end and after that it...it wasn't very easy to...

Pietro, watching her throughout this speech, was appalled by what he saw. Questions rushed to his lips and he choked them back. Later; for the moment, it was enough to recognise that she—like himself—was being driven by necessity. She would not ride on a machine of that kind, so many miles, unless something compelled her. She was, perhaps, running away...but it was plain to see that she was almost at the end of her resources.

"See—" Pietro went round recovering their fallen property. He dragged the bicycle out of the ditch, handed it to Julia to steady and then stuffed brushes—clean, dusty, muddy or bent brushes into his suitcase. He looked for his hat, saw its crown appearing out of the mud in the ditch, and decided to treat it as abandoned. He opened the suitcase again, selected a clothes brush and, kneeling before Julia, dusted the worst of the dirt from her skirt. He borrowed her handkerchief and cleaned her cuts as best he could and then, ignoring his own lamentable state, flashed his beautiful white teeth at her in his enchanting smile.

"Now, my idea!" he said. "I am sick of carrying this box; if you will take him and sit on the bicycle, I will push you—and him."

"Oh—no! I'll walk," protested Julia. "You can't possibly—"

"Oh, no, no, no, no! That will not do," said Pietro. "We have to push the bicycle and carry the box—yes? So we shall have two birds with one stick—one stone. Why shall we push this bicycle with no one upon it? I am too big, so you cannot push me; so you will sit up on it and I will push you. Now see how well we shall go."

Too tired to argue, grateful beyond words for the thought of progressing, even for a short distance, without having to use any effort, Julia, assisted by her new friend, sat perched side-saddle, the suitcase balanced on the handlebars, while Pietro walked firmly beside her, pushing, guiding the bicycle. It was slow, but it was progress. It would take time, but they would get there.

She let a feeling of relief and repose flow over her. She

117

had knocked a man into a ditch, but instead of the abuse, and worse, which she dreaded, he had proved a forgiving, an understanding man—a benefactor.

A foreigner, she thought, as the rest steadied her nerves and allowed a tiny spark of curiosity to kindle.

"Are you going to Greenhurst?" she asked.

"Yes. Greenhurst. My what you call Headquarters is there—my office. I go there to tell them the names of the ladies who wish to have brushes."

"Will you be able to get other ones for the ones that are spoiled?" she asked, anxiously.

"Of course, of course, of course! If I ask, they will give me more," said Pietro, with a confidence he was far from feeling. But the future was the future; it had never worried him before and it would not worry him now. This little girl—this little miss—still she thought only of him and not of herself. It was extraordinary. She was well brought up, so much was plain; a scarecrow she may look now, but it was clear to see that she was of good family; he knew good family when he saw it— who should not, who had waited all his life on good families?

Questions welled up in him, and went unvoiced. She was alone with him on this lonely road; she was too tired to care, but presently she would remember; if he asked questions about her—her name, her business—she would become alarmed. He must keep between them a distance—not physical, for that was impossible, with his shoulder against hers—but he would speak only of general matters. He would discourse.

118

Pietro discoursed—of Italy, of his native village, of his impending voyage to join his brother in New York.

But discoursing, under the circumstances, was killing work. As Pietro flagged, Julia revived, and so it came about that, bit by bit, mile by mile, he learned more and more of the reason for her being here on a too-large bicycle upon a too-long road. Listening, his heart rose within him, and he forgot his fatigue, forgot his ruined clothes and his ruined prospects, forgot the dusty road and the miles still before them. His body marched, but his spirit knelt—for this, he told himself, this was heroism. This thin child with the freckled face and the unkempt red hair— she was of the stuff that made heroes. Alone, she had set out to save her home. Alone, she was on her way to oppose fate; alone, she meant to battle, to stand up to this sister who so coldly, so heartlessly would throw away that most precious of all gifts—a home. This little creature...a one-woman crusade...Ah! it was magnificent! He, Pietro Faccini, would enrol himself on her side. He would say something to this sister. Only wait; her ears would burn. Before he went out of their lives, he would use his gift of discourse—he would place himself behind this brave, this incomparably courageous little miss, this Julia, this gallant little *signorina.*

The thought banished fatigue; Pietro's speed increased to four miles an hour. On! On! Courage, Miss Julia; here are reinforcements, here an ally, here a humble follower. On...!

Chapter Eight

Miss Cornhill sat in a corner of a third-class carriage and read the book she had brought with her. It was not her habit to interest herself in her fellow passengers; if the light were good enough, she invariably read; if the light were bad, she brought out her knitting, which she could do without eyestrain.

There was only one other traveller in the carriage, but Miss Cornhill wished very much that the girl had not chosen this particular carriage to cry in. Crying in public was something so incredible, so inconceivable in a girl of such obviously good background—of what Miss Cornhill termed True Breeding—that she came to the conclusion that she must have suffered a recent—a very recent bereavement. The fact of her not being in mourning was only another sign of the laxity of the times.

The girl's suitcase slipped off the seat for the second time and Miss Cornhill felt bound to make a suggestion. She spoke in her dry, crisp voice, with its Scottish burr.

"Would it not be better to put that up on the luggage rack?"

"Yes. No," faltered Roselle. "It—it's rather heavy."

"Let us do it together." Miss Cornhill marked her place with a book-mark, and rose. "The rack is the place for it."

"Yes. Thank you," said Roselle, as they sat down again. "You're very kind."

Miss Cornhill bowed and opened her book. No more, she said, as plainly as if she had spoken; our association is now at an end. Crossing her neat ankles, she went on with her reading.

She was an extremely neat person. Neatness, in fact, was the dominant note of her existence; she was neat in figure— even at forty-eight; she was neat in her person and neat in her habits. Her life had been a model of neatness ; she had gone through school winning commendation from all her teachers; her desk and her exercise books were impeccably tidy, her plaits always firm, her tunic uncreased. On leaving school, she had trained as a nurse—trim, starched, hygienic—and had then taken a post, first as a junior, then as Head Matron in a famous school. She had retired at forty-five and now lived in a neat little boarding house in Bournemouth, and kept her tiny room a model of neatness. Life, she used to tell the children under her care during her years at the school, should be regulated; it should be lived tidily, with quietness and self-control. To the neat, she said, and believed, all—life itself—was neat.

Roselle, observing the model of self-control sitting before her, wiped her eyes resolutely and looked out at the familiar scene. So near home—and the nearer she got to it, the more she dreaded what she would find when she reached it. Lucille, viewed from the office in London, had seemed merely a sister—now Roselle remembered that she was something more formidable; a guardian, an arbiter; her journey, embarked upon with the object of talking reasonably to Lucille—a scheme which had seemed so sensible a few hours ago—now seemed the height of unreasonableness. If Lucille agreed not to sell the house, what then? Lucille would go off and get married and where could she, Roselle, find the money to run the house? Work was not enough; if they were to live there, they must eat; expenses must be incurred; bills must be paid. Nicholas would come out of the Army; how much could a man—a boy of his age earn? Perhaps Lucille was right, and living at Wood Mount was a dream that couldn't be realised. Perhaps they would never again live there—perhaps they would all have to go away and live for ever with strangers...

Miss Cornhill, stealing a glance at her travelling companion, saw the tears start afresh, and noted other things: the girl was too thin, and far too pale. There was something about her, a look which Miss Cornhill termed the London look—something out of a packet for breakfast, bolted down; a quick-lunch-counter meal in the middle of the day; no tea, and a boiled egg cooked on a gas ring for supper. She needed a sharp talking to—but Miss Cornhill was by no means disposed to administer it.

The train was a slow one, but Miss Cornhill was not in a hurry—and she was interested in her book. The time went by, and presently the train began to lose speed and she saw the girl get up and reach for her luggage. Miss Cornhill rose quietly to help her down with the heavy case, and as she did so, saw that the girl's face was deadly pale. A little uneasy, she let down the window and glanced at the tiny platform coming into view.

"This doesn't look like a station," she observed.

"No, it isn't. Greenhurst station is a little farther on— this is Greenhurst Halt," explained Roselle, "but it's nearer my home, and I can walk from here. There aren't any buses from Greenhurst to—to where I live."

A little nearer—but there would still, she remembered with a sinking heart, be a good way to walk, and she felt...she felt very giddy.

The train stopped; Miss Cornhill sat down and watched Roselle alight. She was, she saw, the only passenger to do so; the slight young figure had an oddly forlorn look on the deserted platform—for Miss Cornhill noticed there was no sign of a porter.

Then she saw Roselle sway, and her professional instinct took her instantly out of the carriage and to Roselle's side. Her movements were swift, but unflustered; she knew quite well what she intended to do; she must lead the girl to that bench over there and let her sit down to recover herself; there would not be time for more, for she would have to get back to her carriage.

But Miss Cornhill was unacquainted with the train driver's notion of what a halt meant. She reached the bench and made Roselle sit down; she did not wait for thanks, but turned to board the train once more—and saw that it was in motion. A reckless young athlete could, no doubt, have taken a flying leap and boarded it, though at some risk—but Miss Cornhill was neither young nor athletic, and so she stood and watched it go. With it, she realised with a feeling of hopelessness, went her luggage...and her handbag. She was left here, penniless, at a halt at which it was not likely that many trains would stop.

The porter, appearing at length, confirmed her fears. No train would stop here before the next morning; this halt was made for business people coming down from London; there never were any business people who wanted to get off here, he explained, taking off his cap to scratch his head in bewilderment, but there it was; the train halted every day, just in case.

Miss Cornhill went over to Roselle and sat on the bench beside her.

"Are you feeling better?"

"Yes, thank you. I'm terribly sorry—I think I made you lose your train."

"Never mind," said Miss Cornhill with composure. "I shall take the bus to Greenhurst and get another train there. The only thing is..." she hesitated and a spot of colour appeared on her cheeks, "it will be necessary for me to borrow a little money from you. If you will give me your address, I shall know where to return the loan."

"Oh:" Roselle's wide blue eyes opened wider with distress. "I—I have very little money with me. I—"

She stopped; it was no use explaining that she had forfeited her salary in lieu of notice.

A faint flush of anger—anger at finding herself in this situation—appeared on Miss Cornhill's cheeks.

"I am not asking for a large sum," she said frostily, "A pound would be enough to get me home."

"I—I've only got two shillings and eightpence," said Roselle, and produced a tiny purse and opened it in unhappy proof. "But if you wouldn't mind coming home with me, my sister would let you have the money."

Going to a stranger's house on such an errand was the last thing in the world she wished to do, but Miss Cornhill realised that there was no other course open to her. She could not ask the porter for money and she could not walk all the way to Greenhurst—it must be seven or eight miles from here, and her shoes were thin and unsuitable for a long walk on country roads. Even if she got to the station, she would have no money to buy a ticket. There was nothing for it but to accompany this helpless little thing to her home and—distasteful as the idea was—borrow money from her sister.

"Shall we go?" she said.

"Yes."

They would not, Miss Cornhill saw with relief, be carrying the heavy suitcase; this was to be left with the porter for collection, the girl said, by the local carrier. With the small case, they set out along the little lane that led to the main road;

here there would be a bus that would go, Miss Cornhill learned to her chagrin, right into Greenhurst. It was exasperating, but she must keep calm and not allow it to upset her. Nobody, fortunately, was to have met her at her destination; nobody would miss her and become anxious.

"My name is Cornhill—Miss Cornhill," she said, as they walked.

"Mine is Roselle Wayne."

"How do you do? This is a nice part of the country, I think," said Miss Cornhill. "I once passed through—"

She stopped. They had reached the end of the lane; they were on the main road, which stretched wide and empty to right and left of them. No...not empty; a motorbike and side-car could be seen in the distance.

They walked on and suddenly, behind them, they heard the horn of the motor-bike sound, and go on sounding.

It was a dreadful noise—loud, raucous; but there was an urgency about the signal that this girl appeared to recognise. Miss Cornhill saw her turn, and pause, and stare—and then suddenly she had given a cry, and she was running—running towards the motor bike with tears pouring down her face...

Perhaps, thought Miss Cornhill, hopefully, perhaps this young man would have a pound or two...

Nicholas had stopped beside them; he had seized Roselle's hands in his and was babbling a string of questions, and listening to an incoherent and tearful account of how she came to be here.

She was on her way home; she, like himself, had felt impelled to come home and fight Lucille. The thought warmed him; he looked at her with a secret sense of shame at having felt, sometimes, that she lacked spunk. Spunk? She was full of it! Walked out of her job, thrown her salary back in her boss's face, hopped on a train and come home to stand up to Lucille.

He acknowledged, somewhat absently, the introduction to her companion. Cornhill; how d'you do. Well, she looked too stiff in the joints to have done anything as impulsive as leaping out of a train to hold up a fainting girl. Not at all the kind, he would have said. He listened to her short and concise summary of the situation.

"And so," she ended, "I was on my way to your home to borrow a little money to enable me to finish my journey. But now that we have met you, it will not be necessary for me to worry your sister; if you will very kindly advance me a pound or two, I shall go straight on to Greenhurst station."

"A..." Nicholas dived instinctively for his money, and then stopped short and coloured deeply. His look told Miss Cornhill that he was as useless in this matter as his sister had been.

"I'm terribly sorry," he said. "I—you see, I bought this bike to-day, and it cleaned me out. But look—you just pop into that side-car, and you, Roselle, can sit behind me and ride pillion. We'll be home in a couple of seconds, and we'll prise the dough out of Lucille."

Miss Cornhill disliked the light tone, the careless term

and, most of all, the low slung, sled-like container into which Nicholas was already assisting her. But it would, after all, get them quickly to the house—and then she could enlist this young man's services to drive her to the station, to her train, and then she would return to her own quiet, orderly life.

She sat with as much dignity as possible in the little seat; Roselle perched herself behind Nicholas and clasped his waist; the engine gave a sound that almost blew Miss Cornhill's hat from her head, and they were off. Miss Cornhill, clutching her hat, her scarf, her hair, glanced at Roselle, and saw her smiling lips and transformed face—and then the side-car went into a canter and her thoughts became fixed solely upon the subject of self-preservation.

Chapter Nine

Dominic's train did not stop at the Halt; when it drew up at Greenhurst Station, he got out, and, forgetful of the fact that Simon had carried the tickets, fished in his pocket at the barrier; finding nothing, he was about to explain matters to his old friend the ticket-collector, when he heard his name called, and looked up to see Simon coming towards him. Beside him was a tall stranger whose face, nevertheless, seemed to Dominic to be vaguely familiar.

"Were you all right?" asked Simon.

"Yes. A lady gave me some tea. How did you come?"

"Mr. Debrett brought me in his car." Simon looked up, and Robert Debrett looked down at Dominic.

"Well," he said. "And so here we all are. Let's go home, shall we?"

He was anxious to witness the end of the affair. They had left without permission, and arrived without warning; this sister, Lucille, was going to get a nice little surprise, and he would like to be there when she got it; he would not judge unseen, but he had what he thought must be a fairly accurate mental picture of her—old for her years, probably; good-looking, if these youngsters were anything to go by, but lacking in imagination or enterprise. Marrying and clearing out. It would be an unhappy ending...

It was nothing to do with him—but he was going to take the boys home and deliver them safely; having handed them over, he was going to wait until Simon had said his piece; he had said it more than once on the way here, fearlessly and sensibly; if he faltered when facing Lucille, he, Robert Debrett, would put in his oar—would speak a few plain words before taking his departure—or being shown the door. Her ears would burn....

They walked out to the road, and Dominic looked up at his brother's new friend; more and more, the feeling of having seen him before pressed upon him.

They went towards the car, and Dominic looked at it with a singular lack of interest.

"Rolls, isn't it?" he said, but his gaze was not on the car. It went from Robert Debrett's face to the huge poster outside the station—and from the poster back to Robert.

"Oh...yes!" he said slowly. "I knew I knew your face. That's you, isn't it?" he said, and jerked his chin backward.

"Yes," said Robert.

Dominic turned to his brother.

"Didn't you *know* that was him?" he asked in surprise.

"No.' Simon coloured. "No, I...I didn't."

"'Course you didn't." Dominic's face cleared. "You didn't go; I went with Aunt Mary." He turned to Robert. "I only saw you in one picture, but you act in lots, don't you?"

"Yes, in lots," admitted Robert.

It was a pity to be recognised now, he thought, for Simon had been unaware of his identity, and oblivious of the stares of the other customers at the Cafe in which they had had tea. But Dominic, to his relief, appeared, now that the question of like-nesses was solved, to have transferred his interest to the car. The three of them got into the front seat, and Dominic, sitting between the other two, volunteered to act as guide.

"Straight on," he directed, "till I say turn."

It was not spectacularly beautiful country, Robert thought, but it was nice and open—and quiet; remote. The town was not pretty, but it was pleasant; his passengers pointed out the shops they knew so well, and he saw the house agent's where somebody called Jeff worked with his father; Jeff, who seemed, from the artless remarks dropped by Simon on the way here, to be a particular friend of another sister named Roselle. Things were piecing together: starting at the top, there was Lucille; then came Nicholas, National Service; Roselle, London busi-ness girl; Julia, schoolgirl—and then these two. A nice-sound-ing lot; a lot, he would have said, to be kept together.

Well, it was not his affair, but he was going to see as much of it as possible now that he was here, now that he had been drawn in so far.

"There's our gate," said Dominic, suddenly.

There was no sign of a house; it must be in those woods over there, thought Robert. Ahead was a wide gateway, and he was preparing to turn into it when it struck him that for a thoroughfare that had seemed, since they left the town of Greenhurst, to have been constructed solely for their own use, there was now an astonishing amount of traffic. A bicycle had just reached the gateway; a motorbike and side car was approaching noisily from the other direction. Perhaps...no, it couldn't be...but perhaps Simon and Dominic weren't the only homing pigeons; perhaps—

Robert had not time to complete this thought. The scene, hitherto one of calm and order, changed without warning into a series of calamities. Dominic, up to now a model, even a phlegmatic passenger, stared at the girl sitting on the bicycle and reared himself up with a loud yell: "JULIA!" The girl, after craning her neck to look at the occupants of the car, opened her mouth and, hurling herself off the bicycle, rushed at the car waving her arms wildly. Swerving to avoid her, Robert found the motorbike bearing down on him and, as he wrenched the wheel over, he saw the machine part and become two separate entities, the motor bike continuing to come straight on and the side car performing a crazy solo all over the road. Robert, as expert a driver as could be found, and equal to any emergency, found this one something beyond normal experience. It was impossible, he saw, for him to stay on the road and avoid running into either the motor bike, its errant side-car, or the bicycle which a man was attempting to drag out of the way. His only course lay in removing himself from their path, and this he proceeded to do: he headed for the ditch, swung the wheel and took the dip as gently as he could; the car lurched, heaved and then sank slowly on to its side.

"You two all right?" asked Robert.

They were both on top of him, but nobody was hurt. Nicholas could be seen looking down at them, struggling with the door; he opened it, and pulled them out one by one, facing Robert at last with an expression of almost ludicrous penitence.

"I'm damn sorry," he said. "The blasted thing came in two.

"It's all right," Robert turned to run an eye over his car. "It won't do it much harm. How's everybody else?"

Everybody but Miss Cornhill had come off without a scratch, but she was lying on the grassy bank on to which the side-car had climbed before overturning and spilling her out. She was on her back, her face to the sky and her expression one of puzzled resignation. As Nicholas ran to her and knelt beside her, she moved her eyes, but seemed unable to turn her head towards him. White faced, he spoke to her falteringly.

"Are you...how d'you feel?" he enquired.

"I...perhaps it's my back," said Miss Cornhill. "I—I don't seem able to...to move."

Nicholas looked at the circle of faces now looking down at Miss Cornhill, and his eyes met Robert's with an agonised question. Robert knelt beside him and passed a swift, exploring hand over her limbs.

"Try to sit up," he urged gently.

"I...I can't."

An expression of bewilderment chased apprehension from Nicholas's face. He had seen the side-car mount the bank; it had taken the rise gently and overturned slowly; then why—?

"Put a hand under her," Robert said, "and ease her up—slowly."

Nicholas slipped a hand gently under Miss Cornhill's back and encountered something hard. Groping, he found that it was the windscreen of the side-car; tracing its outlines, he located half of it wedged firmly beneath Miss Cornhill's coat; the other half was caught in the thick hedge. Miss Cornhill's immobility was explained.

They got her up and Pietro dusted her down, using his finest brush. Nothing could be done to repair her torn coat or her split shoulder-seams, and only time would remove the shame of feeling her hair hanging in wisps about her brow.

Nicholas led the company on to the road and surveyed them. Roselle looked at him and realised that he had changed greatly—he was not the slim, boyish Nicholas who had gone abroad two years ago; he was even taller, and far broader—and immeasurably surer. He looked, and he was behaving, like the head of the family.

It was not a time for questions; it was enough to know that

Miss Cornhill, Robert Debrett and the odd character with the Roman nose and the thick black curls were all benefactors— but this was not the time for thanks. They all needed a rest, and some food—and before all and above all, they needed baths. A dirtier crew, Nicholas thought, he had never seen anywhere.

He led them through the gateway and along the drive; Roselle walked beside him, Julia followed with Simon and Dominic, and the three new friends of the family formed the rearguard.

The house came into view, and Robert's eyes narrowed; this was something unexpected. He hadn't thought much, he realised, about the kind of house it would be; he had looked at it through the eyes of Simon and Dominic, seeing it only as a home—a symbol. But now it stood before him, pale and graceful and lovely, and his interest in the affairs of the Waynes sharpened and deepened.

Miss Cornhill looked at the house with relief; she had not known quite what to expect; two of its members had been travelling with scarcely a penny to their name...it did not reassure one...But this was extremely satisfactory; she could put away her misgivings; with its charming pillars, its graceful flight of steps, this house had something she recognised and saluted: trimness, neatness, grooming.

Pietro liked the house because it looked unlike the usual English country house, which he secretly considered very gloomy. This looked very different—this was a bright house, and a happy house; a patrician house.

He had been right, he reflected; the little miss Julia might be disguised in torn and dirty clothes and have a plain and freckled exterior, but he, Pietro, had not made soup for the daughters of the great for nothing. He had eyes.

Nicholas brought his company to a halt a short distance from the front door.

"I think it would be best," he said, "if I went in alone and had a word with Lucille—with my sister. What d'you say, Roselle?"

Roselle was unable to say anything. Her glance had fallen on the little car standing at the foot of the long flight of steps; it was a new car, and she had not seen it before— but Lucille had no car, and so it must be...It might, of course, belong to Lucille's fiancé, but it was more likely to be...

"Jeff must be here," said Nicholas. "Good."

"Why good?" Julia wanted to know.

"Because I can talk sense to him and he'll listen, even if Lucille won't. Now look—"

He stopped. The door had opened and the newcomers had a momentary glimpse of Jeff beginning to take his leave of Lucille. Then Lucille's glance went past him and, putting him aside slowly, she came out on to the steps like a sleep-walker, her eyes staring down at the company assembled below. Her lips opened, but no sound came.

"Hello, Lucille—we're home," said Nicholas.

He went up the steps in two bounds, took her in his arms

and kissed her lingeringly, and Robert Debrett, watching him, felt an unfamiliar sensation and examined it with some misgiving.

Then, with astonishment, he identified it: for the first time in his spectacularly successful career, he was watching another man play a role he coveted.

Chapter Ten

The next few hours were busy ones for everybody. Fires had to be stoked to provide extra bath water; garments had to be shared out among those who needed them, food had to be prepared. There was no question of the visitors going to other quarters; Miss Cornhill, though now able to borrow money, could not travel until her own clothes were repaired or others obtained for her. Pietro was fitted out in a suit belonging to Nicholas; Robert was still immaculate, but his car gave him the excuse he needed for staying, and he seized it firmly. He was in this thing—well in—and he was enjoying it. He would have to go soon—but not to-night.

In the meantime, they could all make themselves useful. Miss Cornhill would have liked to be upstairs seeing to the children's baths and clothes, but she felt that on this, their only night with Lucille, she should leave them together. She therefore turned her energies to providing supper, and found her way to the kitchen, to discover that Pietro was already there, peering distractedly into drawers and cupboards and assembling the results of his search on the kitchen table. He greeted Miss Cornhill with an exasperated wave of his arms.

"Here there is nothing," he said. "I tell myself that I shall make a good dinner for everybody, and where is the things to prepare? Look."

Miss Cornhill looked. On the table were three tins of baked beans, three tins of sardines, two loaves of bread, a packet of butter and a dozen eggs—Jeff's response to Lucille's request to him to lay in a few provisions for her use during her stay at Wood Mount.

"I plan a little thing—my little speciality," went on Pietro. *"Terrine* of duck—but where shall I get everything? I need so little, but it is not here: how I do it, I shall tell you. A duck—large, of course; the feet of a calf and some pork, and one or two things more—some red wine, some brandy, thyme, spice to mix, onions, garlic, shallots, some—"

"You can put the beans on toast," suggested Miss Cornhill.

"Beans on...! But who will eat that?" Pietro shuddered. "If there is no duck, give me chicken," he besought; "two chickens, and I will make my *Poulet à la Madame Pompadour*; this perhaps will be better for the children. But I shall want ham and some veal—soft, soft veal—and some mushrooms. But of course, mushrooms. Brandy and a little champagne—how can it hurt children, just a little-little? And then I shall need to have—"

"Or you could see," said Miss Cornhill, who had given the matter further thought, "if there were any potatoes in the garden and boil them and mash them up with the sardines—it makes them go a surprisingly long way. Or—' '

"Sardines...mashed with—! But no! How shall we eat that? You see me here," declared Pietro passionately, "ready to cook. For my little Miss Julia, a *gâteau*...yes! *Gâteau Pêche d'Artagnan*. With some ice and some—"

"If you will try to be practical, Mr. er—"

"Pietro, Pietro, Pietro. But I must cook!" he declared. "And see, Mees, how little is there to take for my use! Where is the store place here? Where is the—"

"We weren't expected, and there's nothing to eat."

"But this—ah, yes!" Pietro's smile broke out like sunshine. "This young man, this Jeff—he will have to get food. I will find him."

Jeff was found and despatched into Greenhurst; the shops would be closed, but he must beg or borrow, declared Pietro. Just some little things: a duck or some chickens; ham, pork, veal, wine, brandy, peaches for the *gâteau* for Mees Julia, some tender young peas—very young, very tender; fresh shrimps or prawns for a little cocktail, perhaps—but above all the peaches; ripe, luscious for Mees Julia, nothing could be too good.

Jeff returned with more sardines and more beans; Nicholas had dug potatoes from the garden; Mrs. Milward sent butter and bacon and more eggs. With all this, Pietro had to be content; he set to work with spirits only momentarily dashed, and planned to raise the standard of living as soon as he could get a word with Lucille. Robert, whose object was for the moment to avoid Lucille, appointed himself Pietro's assistant with the idea of keeping out of her way.

Lucille was upstairs with the children. As she went from one member of the family to the next she began to gather at last, out of the confusion, some idea of the upheaval which her letters—her short, swiftly written, carelessly-posted letters had caused.

As yet, she had no comment to make. Nicholas watched her with a wary eye, saying little, but preparing himself, Robert saw, for the struggle that was to come. For the moment, there was too much to be done.

Jeff, returning with the food, had brought an invitation from his mother of accommodation for two people. No two people seemed disposed to come forward to accept the invitation, and although Lucille dropped what she felt was a strong hint to Robert, she found him apparently oblivious; he was either stupid, she thought, or too famous-film-and stage-star to understand that this was not one of his fan clubs. But he had been good to Simon, and she could not seem ungrateful.

She felt too dazed to think clearly about anything. She had spent the afternoon completing, with Jeff, the formalities necessary to the sale of the house; throughout their interview, he had shown clearly that he considered she was acting unwisely, but the criticism was wordless and she had ignored it. She was not doing this, she told herself hardily, because she wanted to, but because she believed it to be for the best—for all of them.

141

Roselle was settled, Nicholas would fend for himself—and the money would provide a start for him in civilian life. She would have a home to offer the children—Digby had from the first shown a touching generosity over the question of inviting them to spend their holidays with them. He had understood the situation; he had sympathised with her over its difficulties, and agreed as to the wisdom of the sale.

This unlooked-for development, this shattering, unexpected response to her letter, brought back all her doubts and uncertainties—but nothing could come of it, she decided, except a disagreeable interlude of argument and protest. None of them would have any feasible proposition to put forward; they wanted to keep the house, but they could not provide the money with which to do it. She dreaded the morning, when Nicholas would—she could see—present the case.

But the morning was the morning; let it wait. In the meantime, there was supper, and as she looked round the table, she came to the conclusion that she was dreaming; they were not really here; it was something she had built up in her mind, the result of worrying too much over the house. But they looked real enough: Miss Cornhill, dignified in spite of torn seams; Robert Debrett, calm and—she couldn't help thinking—completely at home; Pietro, dancing in and out of the dining-room bearing dishes which—from his reverent handling of them—might have contained caviar, but which turned out to be full of baked beans.

The telephone shrilled as they went into the hall, and Lucille went over to answer it. Some instinct drew Simon to her side; the others waited where they stood, frankly listening; Lucille, looking them over, saw that there was a quite unmistakable eve-of-battle look about them; nobody knew, as yet, who was on which side, but everybody— even the prim Miss Cornhill—showed clearly that a telephone call was now a matter of general and not merely family interest.

"Greenhurst two-four," said Lucille. "Yes...yes, Aunt Mary...yes, they are." A faint flush crept into her cheeks. "I was going to ring you up as soon as...Yes, they...I beg your pardon?...Yes...Yes, I see...Well, that, of course, is entirely up to you." The flush deepened; the tone, from one of warmth and reassurance, had grown formal and chill. "Yes, certainly; you must do as you please. Yes...Good-bye."

She put down the receiver, her brows drawn in anger. There was a short silence, and then Simon was heard clearing his throat nervously. Dominic came over to join him, and Lucille looked down at them; it became clear that her anger was not directed against them.

"Was that..." Simon looked up at her. "I suppose that was Aunt Mary?"

"It was," said Lucille.

"Did she...I mean, did she sound...cross?"

"Not at all," said Lucille calmly. "She sounded relieved."

"What for, relieved?" asked Dominic, puzzled.

"Because you're not going to live with her any more,"

143

said Lucille in the same even tones.

"We're..." Dominic turned for enlightenment to Simon and the latter, torn between apprehension and relief and showing both emotions clearly on his face, tried to explain.

"They've—they've chucked us out, I expect," he said.

"You mean for *good*?"

"Yes—have they, Lucille?"

"You mean we can't go *back* there?" shrilled Dominic.

"Can we, Lucille?" asked Simon.

"You can NOT."

"Oh." An expression of deep relief came into Simon's face. "Oh...*jolly* good..."

"Oh, jolly good, jolly good, jolly hopping good." chanted Dominic. "Now that beastly baby can howl all day if it wants to, and I shan't have to talk to it and make it go to sleep. I'm jolly glad, and I bet Simon is too—aren't you, Simon?"

Simon, glancing at Lucille's face, decided that this was not the moment in which to express his satisfaction. He moved close to Roselle and she took his hand and squeezed it affectionately. Lucille's eyes rested on them, and she addressed Roselle.

"What happened to your job?" she said.

"I gave notice," said Roselle.

"After you'd got my letter?"

"Well, I wanted to give notice in any case," said Roselle. "I—I gave a week's notice in lieu of salary."

"Vice versa," prompted Jeff, in an undertone, from behind her.

"But I don't understand," said Lucille, "why you—"

She paused. The telephone bell had shrilled again. This time, she made no attempt to answer it. She looked at Nicholas.

"I think you'd better," she said.

Nicholas lifted the receiver.

"Yes? Speaking, yes...Yes, Sister, she's here. Yes, I—But I can assure you that...You see, I...Yes, Sister...Yes, Sister... Yes, Sister...Yes, Sister."

He replaced the receiver, his face expressionless. Julia crept to his side.

"Wasn't that..." She stopped.

"Yes, Sister," said Nicholas.

"Oh. I mean, was she..."

"Yes, Sister. You're expelled."

It took time to penetrate.

"I'm...what am I?"

"You're expelled," repeated Nicholas. "You're sacked. You're out—for good. You've got the boot; the push; the air; the brush-off. Briefly, you're expelled."

Julia stood rigid for a few moments and then gave vent to a curious, low moan. Her wild glance round the room showed that the four walls were insufficient to contain her emotions. The others were at the front door, on their way out to the greater freedom of the garden, and with a wild shriek, she rushed to join them. There was a swooping movement of her red head; it vanished, and in its place appeared two skinny legs which wavered in the air and then steadied and remained stiff as Julia joined the procession and walked out—on her hands.

The door closed on a vision of deplorable bloomers. Lucille, without speaking, walked into the drawing-room, and after a moment, Robert came to the door and stood watching her. She picked up a cigarette box and held it out. Not until their cigarettes were lighted did he break the silence. Then he glanced across at her expressionlessly.

"Well," he said. "You seem to have run into some complications, don't you?"

☙

"They are nice, no?" confided Pietro to Robert later, as they washed the dishes together.

"Very nice."

"Those children—so sweet."

"Yes."

"And they are all so beautiful, no? All except Miss Julia, I think—but she will grow different in some years."

"No doubt."

"I like this family already. I feel one with them—here," said Pietro, the handle of a wooden spoon indicating his heart. "I am lonely for my brothers and sisters all the time. The big family, how good it is, no?"

"I daresay," said Robert.

Lucille was upstairs gathering more news items as she put the children to bed.

"But, Simon, didn't you say *anything* to them?"

"I left a letter for Aunt Mary. I said we were here, and not to worry about us. I left it in the kitchen and I put a milk bottle on it so's it wouldn't blow away."

"But...you could have *written* to me!"

"No, we couldn't. We wanted to see you, and—and so we came. But there was an awful crowd on the station when we got there from Shrewsbury, and Dominic got carried away by the people, and I couldn't see him"— Simon paused to stare at the horrid memory—"and then Mr. Debrett picked me up so's I could make signs to Dominic and tell him to go on. Then he brought me here in his car."

"Did you know who he was?"

"No. Dominic knew. Dominic had seen him—I think I had too, once, only I'd forgotten. He was awfully nice, Lucille. He gave me tea and two ices, and when his car went into the ditch, he didn't seem to mind." There was a pause and then, "Lucille—"

"In the morning, Simon," she said hastily, at the new note in his voice. To-morrow they would argue it out— not to-night.

She found Julia entirely unmoved at the thought of Belinda's feelings, or her parents' anxiety, or Mr. Penley's loss; Belinda would guess why she went, her parents had simply lost their nerve and given her away—and Mr. Penley would get the remains of his bicycle back in the morning. The only one who was causing her any anxiety was Signor Faccini.

"He must have hurt himself when I thudded into him, Lucille—but he didn't say a word; he just got out and picked up his brushes and then he made me sit on the saddle while he pushed and pushed, for miles! And he made jokes— and he sang, and he made me sing, and then I didn't feel tired any more—but his brushes are spoiled, and we'll have to buy him some new ones, won't we?"

"Yes. But Julia—"

"I know you think I came because of my books, Lucille, but I didn't—not really. It was Long John."

"Long John.

"I know he's Simon's, but I knew Simon wouldn't say anything, and just go on feeling bad about him. You said a year—you told us all it would only be a year—"

"I said we'd try it for a year, Julia. You can't always do what you want to do in this world. You have to—"

"Even if we could understand, Long John wouldn't. Dogs don't forget—Mr. Hewett said so. He said Long John would remember. And then there was the tree house—how could anybody move a tree house?"

"We'll talk about it in the morning, Julia. Not now."

It was hardest of all to understand Roselle.

"You mean...you can't mean that you *never* liked it? You

148

were so madly keen to go, Roselle—you wanted to live there and to work there."

"But I didn't know what it would be like in London. I'd only been on visits before. I didn't know what it would be like all the year round—just sitting in that awful office and in that awful room and..."

"But you could have written to me—long ago. You could have told me, and I could have got a day off and come up to see you, and talk to you. It didn't have to be London, if you wanted a job and independence; it could have been somewhere near me in Cornwall. It could still be somewhere near me."

"It was being away from home. How can you know, until you go away, what it'll be like without a home? I didn't like to worry you because I knew you were just as worried about it all as I was—I knew that if you could have us all home again, you would. I didn't know you'd meet someone and..."

"He's very nice, Roselle—he's kind and he knows all about you all and he's longing to meet you. My home will be your home, too."

No answer. And no spark of enthusiasm, Lucille noted. This was all going to be more than she could cope with. A dull feeling of depression settled on her.

Her thanks to Miss Cornhill were cut politely, but firmly, short. Miss Cornhill was, in fact, far too busy to listen; there was work to be done and she was secretly amazed at the pleasure she was finding in doing it. Something within her that had been struggling for release had now welled up, and she knew that her two years of retirement had been rather dull ones. She was back at work—familiar work—congenial work; she was extraordinarily happy.

Lucille left her and went to seek out Pietro. Her speech of thanks to him was interrupted while he took over and gave her a flowery and picturesque but distressingly detailed description of the state in which he had found Julia. Lucille listened and looked at his expressive hands, his large, flashing eyes and his thick black curls, and wondered once more whether she was dreaming.

Robert Debrett, after their brief encounter in the drawing room, was proving difficult to get hold of; if there were any reason for avoiding her, Lucille would have thought that he was doing so.

She found him at last in the kitchen, putting away the dishes; there was no sign of Pietro. This time her thanks were neither cut short nor snatched from her and returned with flowers; Robert merely listened attentively until she came to a somewhat faltering end.

"You mustn't thank me," he said at last. "I enjoyed it very much."

She looked at him; he was acting, she knew, but why would he act now—unless it were from force of habit?

"You can't have enjoyed having your car wrecked," she said with a flash of irritation. "I went out to look at it. It's a Rolls, and it's lying in a ditch. Where's the enjoyment?"

He gave her what with rising anger, she felt the film director would call a hooded glance.

"Your brothers," he told her quietly, "are charming. And very plucky."

She caught herself up on the point of asking him why they were plucky; his manner seemed to indicate that they were plucky to come and face her. A sense of injustice rose in her and he saw for the first time what Mr. Milward had so often seen and deplored—the too-swift rise of her temper.

"They ran away," she said. "What's plucky about that?"

"Your letter was a challenge. They rose to it—beautifully."

"I think you've rushed to one or two unfortunate conclusions, Mr. Debrett," she said. "The question of our selling, or not selling the house isn't a new one; we've been over it many times before."

"I hope you'll go over it again."

"And I hope you won't look for too much drama in a quite straightforward situation. This thing has many sides and you've only seen one of them."

He turned to study her—a long, speculative look—and she felt her anger increasing. He saw her—of course he would, after spending those hours with Simon and Dominic—he saw her as the hard, selfish eldest sister throwing the home to the dogs and going off to find happiness for herself.

A longing to push his head under the cold tap before

which they were standing filled her, and showed clearly on her face. Robert watched her and smiled happily to himself. This was going to be livelier than he had anticipated.

She opened her mouth to speak, and he waited with keen interest—but the door had opened, and Miss Cornhill had come into the room.

"I wonder," she asked Lucille, "if you could tell me whether there are any hot water bottles in the house? I think the children would go to sleep more quickly tonight, after all this excitement, if they had one each. If you could—"

She stopped abruptly, her face paling. "W—What is that noise?" she asked.

"It's all right," said Lucille. "That's only my brother, Nicholas, giving off a trumpet solo."

"Ah," said Miss Cornhill.

"Virtuoso," commented Robert. "He's quite a—my God, what's that?"

They listened.

"I think," said Lucille slowly at last, "that it must be Pietro...singing."

"Suffering tomcats," murmured Robert, whether as an ejaculation or a comparison was not clear. "I'll go up and choke him."

"Hello," said Nicholas, as he went in. "Too much row here?"

"Yes. I thought Pietro was with you."

"He was—until he joined in. Now he's in the garden looking for—I think—rare herbs."

"I've rung up the breakdown gang," said Robert, sitting on the bed. "They'll be out to-night. Is your motor bike a total loss?"

"The bike's all right, and I never wanted a side-car anyway. I bet Miss Cornhill never took a ride like that before. My gosh"—Nicholas laid down his trumpet— "she gave me a fright, lying there with a presumably cracked spine, and preparing to dictate codicils. Bad moment, that. I did tell you I was sorry about your car, didn't I?"

"Yes—several times. Between you and me, nothing could have turned out more fortuitously."

"Nice word; what's it mean?"

"It means that I'm glad I'm here."

"You won't be in the morning. There's going to be a large-scale attack against Lucille—and you can see, now that you've met her, that we'll only be five to one—which isn't enough. You taking sides?

"Yes."

Nicholas whistled.

"No—really? Hers or ours?"

"Mine and mine only. Your sister and I had a brief interview a moment ago, and I came out of it with less than full marks. The look on her face as I left said clearly, 'This man must go'—and this man is bent on staying."

"You must have it wrong" said Nicholas, after consideration. "You're the boy the girls all pant after. We're not what you'd call theatrically-minded, as a family, but even Lucille must have heard of you, and what girl would tell her friends she only had you in the house for a short time? You must have read the signs wrong."

"I never read signs wrong," said Robert calmly.

"Well, for myself, I'd be glad to have you around when the storm breaks," said Nicholas frankly. "You give me confidence somehow, I don't know why. The Cornfield's no use; I've upset her life, and ruined her travelling suit, and I daresay she'll hold it against me. The Italian's less than useless; if he's present at all—which we'll try to prevent—he'll make long speeches about how beautiful Julia is going to be in a few years—odd thought, isn't it, when you look at her now But you...you're a sensible age and you've got a sensible look and the two boys like you. You could stand behind me and prop me up every time I look like sagging."

There was silence; as it lengthened, some of the brightness went out of Nicholas's face.

"What's the matter?" he asked at last. "Don't you feel we've got a case?"

Robert propped a pillow behind his back and made himself comfortable before answering.

"You've got a good case," he said thoughtfully, "but as I see it, you're going into court a bit unprepared. All the emotional—the sentimental factors are in your favour, but your sister is basing her arguments on solid facts. I hate to seem to butt in on your—"

"Skip it. Go ahead and help me. You're right—I'm only *feeling* this thing instead of thinking it."

"Yes. As I understand it, you can't keep the house because you haven't the money to run it."

"At the moment we haven't; agreed. But blast it, I've only just come out of the Army! I didn't buy the bike for pleasure—there was a strictly practical idea behind it: I had an idea that if I could get a job in Greenhurst, I could tool myself to and fro every day—there's no bus service. If I get a job, if Roselle runs the house, that's something, isn't it? It's a start. Not that I'll earn much at first, but all we need, for the moment, is money enough to meet the food bills and the rate bills. You don't just chuck a home away because you're short of money. You look at your potentials, don't you? You list your assets; you see where you can rake in dough. Isn't that right?"

"Your sister's going to be married, and—"

"Well, let her. Let her go to this Digby character and marry him and raise little Digbees; nobody's stopping her. All we're asking is for time, that's all; time to organise. She's worked so fast that there were people coming to look at the house tomorrow—think of it, tomorrow! She can't *do* that! She—"

"Pietro's coming back," said Robert, sitting upright and glancing out of the window. "Look, Nicholas, don't worry too much—we'll work out something. If there's a fight—which I hope there won't be—I'll come in on your side."

"Thanks. The real fighter," said Nicholas moodily, picking up his trumpet once more, "is young Julia. If Julia were older, she could handle Lucille. I could handle Lucille—if she were a man instead of a girl."

Robert said nothing. He could, he thought, handle Lucille—in spite of being a man.

Chapter Eleven

Lucille slept little that night, but before she slept she had come to a decision: she would telephone to Jeff in the morning and ask him to come out and drive her in to see his father some time during the morning.

With the thought of seeing Mr. Milward, and hearing his slow, sensible sentences, she felt better; she felt able to face the coming struggle with Nicholas with all her usual coolness.

Nicholas rose late and went into the kitchen to watch Pietro cooking him a hearty breakfast. There was no sign of any of the others; Dominic and Julia could be heard up in the tree house; Simon had vanished after breakfast; Robert Debrett was somewhere in the garden, and Roselle was tidying rooms with Miss Cornhill.

Nicholas ate to the accompaniment of Pietro's story of his life. It began with the porridge, cooked as a Scotsman had once shown Pietro how to cook it; it went on through bacon and eggs and was brought up to date with the marmalade. Nicholas chewed and listened with equal enjoyment; they were alone, said Pietro, they were in this nice kitchen to themselves, and he would leave out nothing. Nothing.

"Such a happy life!" he sighed, reaching for Nicholas's cup and filling it yet again. "And still there is more to come; I am young; I have plenty to go. There has never been money, but what is money?"

Money, reflected Nicholas, was pretty well everything. For him and for his family at the moment, it meant this house and this way of life; the difference between unity and separation. He would not, two years ago, have thought of the Waynes as a united family; yesterday's return of his sisters and brothers had moved him more than he cared to admit, and he felt ready for Lucille and any opposition she cared to put forward.

He sought her out after breakfast and found her in the bathroom, washing the less bulky of the garments Julia had come home in. He came in, kicked the door shut, sat on the edge of the bathtub, and began without preamble.

"Well, what about it, Lu?"

"If you mean the house," she said, without pausing in her work, "I'll talk about it later. Jeff's calling for me soon and taking me in to see Uncle Bill."

"This is nothing to do with Jeff or Uncle Bill," pointed out Nicholas. "This is purely our affair. Look, I've got a proposition; let me take over the house."

She turned from the basin, dripping hands idle, to stare at him.

"I don't understand."

"It's very simple: You're getting married—incidentally,

congratulations, and I hope you'll be very happy, and I think he's a lucky guy if he doesn't knuckle under. Well, as I say, you're marrying him; he's been very kind and said we can look in on you at any time, but we want to be here, in our own home, Lu, and not in yours. We—"

"I've—"

"Hold it; one at a time, and you don't know what I'm going to say, yet. I propose that you go ahead with your life— which is right and proper—and let me take on this house and the kids."

"And support them on what?"

"I can get a job in Greenhurst."

"A third-rate, run-of-the mill, small-man job in a—"

"Small town; yes, that's why I want to start there. We're known here in Greenhurst, Lu; in any other place, I'd just be another ex-Army guy looking for a job; here in Greenhurst I'm Mr. Wayne of Wood Mount. Not much, certainly—outside Greenhurst—but in Greenhurst quite a pull...And as to third rate...Jeff hasn't done so badly, sticking down here with his father. It may have looked unenterprising—I used to think it was, but now I don't any more. If I didn't get in anywhere else, Uncle Bill would find a place for me in his office—but I will find something. No, don't say anything yet. That's me settled and bringing in a bit. Now Roselle: I know it's only a reaction after London, but she's burning to cook and wash and work in the house, and so instead of wasting this power, I propose to harness it; I want her to run the house for us—and a couple of p.g's—Paying Guests. Lodgers. Boarders."

"You think Roselle can tackle a—"

"Half a mo; boarders. People—some people—would be jolly glad to live out here in the nice, open country, and go into Greenhurst every day. The Bank Manager—the new one; he's a widower and he'd probably jump at it. Uncle Bill knows everybody, and he'd even put up a notice in his office if we wanted him to. No—I haven't done yet. Schools : the boys'll have to be fixed up; Julia'll have to be fixed up. Julia's no problem—she can go as a day girl to Greenhurst. It isn't a Ladies Seminary, exactly, but she always loathed boarding school, and she'll enjoy tooling back and forth on a bicycle—and coming home every day. The boys are more difficult, but I thought I'd pop out myself to see my old Headmaster and talk to him. I'll crawl in on my knees and spill the whole story and see if he can't let 'em in on the, as it were, instalment plan—I pay so much now and more as and when I can afford it. If you help me a bit there, it would be useful, but I don't know how this Digby fellow of yours is placed financially. He's support-ing his mother, isn't he?"

Lucille hesitated.

"No—not exactly. He lives with her—I mean, they're in the house they lived in before his father died; they've just gone on living in it."

"But he has to fork out a bit towards her upkeep, I sup-pose?"

"No. She's got money of her own."

"Well, that helps; I mean, it might leave you with a bit, and if you sent it along—when you could afford it— we wouldn't proudly spurn it. So there you are; now I've put it to you. I know you don't think I'm up to carrying the weight, but I'm certain I am, and I'm certain it'll work out. Now you can talk."

Lucille did not seem disposed to talk; she was rubbing the clothes once more, but the energy had gone out of her movements. Nicholas watched her, and a new sense of her beauty rose in him and filled him with an indefinable regret. He had looked at her all his life and he had known that he had a pretty sister—but he had accepted the fact with all the other facts concerning his family. It was only lately that he had come to understand that his mother's illness had been a drain on their resources—and upon Lucille's youth; it was only now that he seemed to see the strength and the courage with which she had lived through all those difficult years. He looked at the glory of her hair, the creamy smoothness of her arms. He had lived among men, and he saw her now through their eyes, her full, red lips and lovely face and desirable body. He wondered, for the first time, whether Digby Russell deserved her and her beauty. A stranger—a total stranger; she was leaving them and going to him...

"If you don't mind," said Lucille slowly, "I'll leave it till I've seen Uncle Bill."

"Why? How can he decide this for you?"

"He can assess your chances of making a go of it better than I can—perhaps better than you can."

161

"He'll be on my side."

"Why this talk of sides?" Lucille's voice rose. "This isn't a war—this is a family problem, that's all. And I'm beginning to resent the way I'm represented as the all-time, heavy-footed, bullying head of a bunch of cowering orphans. It's a false picture and you know it."

"I don't know it—yet. Your letter wasn't a proposition, you know; it was a plain statement of fact: we're selling."

"Not from choice—you knew that quite well."

"Not after discussion—I knew that quite well, too. I don't altogether blame you; two years ago, I wasn't much use to you—and neither was Roselle. But you shouldn't have assumed that we wouldn't want a say in things now."

"Roselle couldn't get out of this house fast enough— a year ago. If I'd suggested selling it—then—she wouldn't have had a word to say against the suggestion. Who's to say that in another year she won't have changed her mind again?"

"A year from now," said Nicholas, "she'll be married to Jeff."

She looked at him scornfully.

"No, she won't. She had her chance and she didn't take it. For the past four months, Jeff's been going about with the Arkwright girl. Miriam Arkwright. His mother told me."

"Well, I'm sorry for Miriam, that's all—she's got a big disappointment coming. But with Lord Templeby for a father, she should catch a husband without much trouble. Only it

won't be Jeff. It's interesting to come back, Lu, and find that
you can be as dim as other girls; I've got so used to looking up
to you as the great know-how. Roselle has learned a lot in the
past year. My bet is that after a decent interval to soothe his
pride—and to give Roselle a hell of a fright—Jeff will come
at her again—and then we'll sling the boarders out and he
and she can marry and settle down here; the house will divide
quite well and they can have their own bed-and bath-and-suite.
So take what I've said seriously—and leave me the house and
get married and be happy and don't worry about us. You've
done your whack for this family. I thought a lot when I was
away—and I realised that the years mother was ill were bad
ones for you. You don't have to go on carrying us all; we've all
got our leg muscles now. What's this Digby chap like?"

"He's..." Lucille frowned. It was difficult not to remember that on her first meeting with him, she had been singularly
unimpressed. But she had to remember that it had been at a
tea party and he had come with his mother and handed round
toasted scones—a situation in which few men looked their
strongest.

"He's tall—wears glasses, but they suit him; he's got a
long, rather clever face—in fact, he's a very clever man. He's
kind and—and patient."

"If his mother's got money, why this arrangement of her
living with you when you're married?"

"Well, it seemed pointless for her to move out just because Digby was marrying me. There the house was, and there

163

was all their furniture, and it's one of those large, rather solid, ugly, old-fashioned houses that wouldn't fetch much if they sold it—and so it seemed more sensible for us all to go on living there. There's lots of room—for her and for you all."

Nicholas thought the picture remarkably unattractive, but he said nothing. One thing at a time. He rose and opened the door.

"I'll go into town and see Uncle Bill myself," he said. "And do a bit of scouting round."

"One moment," Lucille closed the door cautiously. "When are all these strays leaving?"

"What—Corny and the chef and Robert? What's the hurry? We owe them something."

"They can't settle down here for ever. If you don't want that suit you lent Pietro, you could donate it to him, couldn't you, and let him go on his way?"

"Then you would have to do the cooking—or Roselle would. Why not leave well alone? He's happy in the kitchen, and Corny's going round the house in a fever, tidying as she goes."

"Well, Robert Debrett isn't cooking and he isn't tidying; you can get rid of him."

"Ah." Nicholas looked at her frowning brows. "Has he said something?"

"He hasn't said anything; I imagine he thinks he doesn't have to; just being around is enough to enchant people— he thinks."

"Oh look, Lu, you've got him all wrong. He's all right."

"He's staying here solely in order to see what we're going to do—and I won't have it. It's nothing whatsoever to do with him."

"It was my fault that he had to ditch his car."

"It isn't in the ditch now, and it isn't hurt—I went out and looked. Besides, he earns fabulous sums—if he wants to hang around, he can go into Greenhurst and get a room at the George."

"But I like him."

"And I don't."

"All right then—you tell him to go."

She made no reply, and after a glance at her angry face, Nicholas went out and, grinning in the safety of the landing, ran downstairs and met Robert in the hall. Taking him by the arm, he led him out into the garden.

"When do you want to go off?" he enquired, in a low voice.

Robert looked at him.

"I don't want to," he said. "Not yet, anyhow. But if I'm in the way—"

"We're all for keeping you as long as you can stay. All but one of us, that is."

"Ah," said Robert. "I'd already gathered that."

"I know. You said so, and you were right. Some people

make it so plain, don't they? You know how you stand with them, at all events. But my advice is to treat a certain person with consummate tact. If you don't give people the opportunity, then they can't, so to speak, serve notice on you, if you follow me."

"If she really feels I'm—"

Nicholas looked pained.

"If you're going to take that gentlemanly attitude, then I'm wasting my time. I didn't tell her so just now, but I have an idea we're stuck with Pietro permanently. He likes us, and keeps saying so. Miss Cornhill will depart in due course—but while she's here, you hang on. We like having you round."

"Thank you."

"Not at all. Want a lift into town?"

"Pillion?"

"Naturally. I can't take you in the side-car unless I tow you."

"I'll stay at home, thanks."

"As you like. Oh—there's one other thing."

"Well?"

"Would you do me a little favour?"

"Yes."

Nicholas grinned appreciatively at the promptness of the reply.

"Well, when Jeff turns up this morning to take Lucille into town," he said, "could you pretend you've got an urgent date with the fellows who're doing your car?"

"Yes. But why?"

"It's only a two-seater, and you could offer to drive Lucille in and bring the car back for Jeff."

"But that leaves Jeff marooned out here."

"Quite right. But you'll find he won't waste his time. Or I hope he won't."

There was a pause while Robert examined all the aspects of this plan. The more he looked into it, the more highly did he rate Nicholas's intelligence.

An hour later, he was seated in Jeff's car, with Lucille beside him, driving towards Greenhurst.

They said little at first. Lucille leaned back, glad to be for a little while out of the house; she was feeling tired and confused. This time yesterday, she had arrived in Greenhurst with a cut-and-dried plan; to-day, she was leaving a house into which all her brothers and sisters had flocked, bringing strangers with them—and she was driving into town with Robert Debrett, the screen's most sought-after bachelor, feeling nothing but irritation at the certainty that he meant to stay and see the affair out to the end. Well, he wouldn't have that satisfaction. This going in to see his car was a good sign; perhaps she was misjudging him, she thought; perhaps she was over-rating his interest in their problem. It was not likely, after all, that a— what was the term?—a popular idol would be able to immure himself in a country house and stay there indefinitely, without causing chaos among his adorers. There was nothing here for him; he had been kind to Simon and Dominic, and she was grateful—he had done a good deed, and he would no doubt have his reward hereafter, but he wasn't— she hoped—going to imagine that his fame entitled him to a special berth for as long as he cared to occupy it. Perhaps she ought to be panting with excitement at this moment, but she hadn't time; her mind was too fully occupied with other things.

"Worried?" enquired Robert presently.

"In a way," she admitted.

"You're lucky to have a nice family like this. I was an only child, and I missed a lot of fun."

"You have quite a lot of fun now, judging from the news-papers."

Her tone was cool, and he found the coolness bracing. This was, he knew, no deliberate withdrawal to make him believe, as some women tried to make him believe, that the glamour of his person and position was having no effect upon them. It was an old ruse and it never worked. This girl really wanted him out of the way; she suspected his motives and re-fused to have him, a stranger, prying into her private affairs. She was right and he was acting reprehensibly in not remov-ing himself at once—but he realised that he wanted, more and more, to stay. There was barely enough excuse for staying, but it was enough: Simon and Dominic liked him, he had brought them home, and in doing so had been deprived of the use of his car. He was ashamed of his lack of delicacy in staying on, and astonished at the dismay with which he regarded his eventual going.

He examined the dismay, and put it down to an instinctive attraction towards the family life that he had missed. This was a real family; a large, a charming family—an interesting family. He wanted to stay with them—just for a little while. He was enjoying himself; he was strangely happy. They all wanted him to stay—all but this girl seated beside him—this lovely red-head. There were a lot of redheads nowadays, but not many natural ones. This girl's beauty would have taken her a long way in his profession; she certainly had the looks...and she certainly had the temperament...

He wanted to talk to her, but he remembered Nicholas's advice, and said as little as possible. She was waiting for an opportunity to trap him into saying he would go; the least said, the better.

Lucille got out at Mr. Milward's office, and Robert drove away to the garage. She stood and looked after him thoughtfully, and then turned and went into the dim little entrance.

Mr. Milward seated her in a chair by the window and heard her out without interruption. He had listened to her, seated just as he was seated now—his chair swivelled sideways, his legs crossed, his glasses now on his nose, now in his hands—he had listened to her impassioned outbursts as a child and her heated complaints as a girl; he had listened, and nodded, and sat silent to the end, and then he had given her, at last, his slow, calm words of advice. She had seldom taken the advice, but the visits had always soothed her; Jeff always showed her in and closed the door upon them both, leaving them in what he termed, on these occasions, the explosion chamber. Lucille emerged feeling much better, and went away with Mr. Milward's blessing to do as she pleased.

His advice this time was unexpected.

"You must send for your fiancé," he said simply.

Lucille stared at him.

"What for?" she enquired.

The question seemed to him an extraordinary one from a woman who was about to take a man as a life partner.

A great many answers came to his mind: for help, for counsel, for guidance—even for comfort. He said none of this, however, and only looked at Lucille mildly.

"You came here to leave the sale of the house in our hands; this return of your brothers and sisters is a complication which is bound to delay you, and you fiancé must be advised."

"What can he do all that way away?"

"I said that you must send for him. This concerns him as well as yourself, Lucille. If you care to telephone from here, perhaps you can get him in his office; you can explain what has happened, and if you don't care to ask him to come, you could leave it to him to decide whether he will do so or not. But you cannot settle this out of hand."

"Nicholas says I can; he says it's nothing to do with anybody else."

"Your decision will be your own, but your fiancé has the right to know what is going on."

"Uncle Bill...is Nicholas's plan..."

"It has a great deal to recommend it."

"But it sounds crazy! How can I just walk out and leave him and Roselle to—to run the place? All he's got in the world is a few pounds, a motor bike and a trumpet. And Roselle's sweet, but what help will she be?"

He put on his glasses and looked at her in silence for some moments.

"You must learn," he said quietly at last, "that you're not in charge of them any more, Lucille. You— One moment!" He held up a long white hand and waited for silence. "You have been splendid all these years; splendid. You looked after your father, and you nursed your mother; more, you took the household on your shoulders for all those years and bore the weight of it. But things have changed now; Nicholas is a man and you can—you must—pass the burden over to him. If you don't, you will be doing him a great wrong. While he was young, while he was away, of course you had to have control—but he's here now, and ready for responsibility; you must give it to him. You don't have to worry, any more, about whether things will work out or not; their success, or their failure will depend on Nicholas's strength—or weakness. You must not deprive him of the right to test himself."

"But—but he hasn't the faintest idea of what running the house entails! He—"

171

"He'll learn."

"And money—where will..."

"He will get a good job here in Greenhurst, and he's extremely sensible to realise it. In fact, I think his whole scheme is full of sound sense. He is known here, and liked—and trusted. This is a progressive little town, and he will do better here—for the present, at any rate—than in a place in which he is unknown. I myself will arrange Julia's entry into the school here and—as Nicholas guessed—I will be able to find suitable paying guests for Wood Mount. You mustn't feel that you're leaving them all entirely without friends, you know. You can go away and live a happy life with your husband; everything will be well here."

He stopped, and there was a long silence. Lucille was staring at him, and he saw there was a strange look on her face. If it had been anybody but Lucille, he would have said that she looked forlorn. Then, to his astonishment, he saw tears spring to her eyes and roll down her cheeks.

She had not cried for years. The last time...how long ago was it? He could scarcely remember. But he had known, in those days, exactly what she was crying about. To-day he did not feel so sure.

He waited for her to explain her distress, but Lucille said nothing until she had taken out a handkerchief and mopped her face angrily.

"My dear," he said gently, "you're not to worry about them."

172

"I'm not w-worrying," sobbed Lucille. "I—I'm just thinking."

"Of the future?"

"N-no." It was a desolate sound. "But everybody— all of you, all you say is Go. Nicholas told me to g-get out—oh, not in so many w-words, but that's what it amounted to. And now you've just said the same thing. Go away. Go and get married. Go away and leave Wood Mount and all of them in it—leave your home, leave your family, and go on down to C-Cornwall and stay there. I kept the home together—you know I did. You just said so. And now you say that all I've got to do is....is walk out and leave it and..."

He got up and walked in his slow, measured way across the room. Standing by her chair, he put his hand on the hair he loved so much and stroked it tenderly.

"It's hard," he said, "but it's life. Besides, Lucille, you're going to a home of your own. Soon you'll have your own children, your own family."

It sounded weak; it was weak, thought Mr. Milward. She wasn't going to a home of her own; she was merely joining her husband and his mother. He wondered, with a recurrence of misgiving, what sort of man this Digby Russell was—and then he realised that he must find out. That, indeed, was the core, the crux of the situation. They must know more of the man Lucille was marrying; they must learn his reaction to the new developments and find out whether he could be of practical use. He might even be able to help them, in a small way,

173

financially. He might back Nicholas; he sounded, at all events, an able man and there was no point in leaving him, unaware, down there in Cornwall. Lucille must telephone.

He waited outside while she put the call through; when she joined him, he thought she was looking better.

"He's coming," she said.

"When?"

"At once."

Mr. Milward gave a small, inward sigh of relief. That sounded reassuring. He did not know quite why he had needed reassurance, but it was good to know that the fellow had acted promptly. Perhaps he was going to prove the man to straighten things out.

"Good," he murmured, and walked to the door with her. "By the way, where's Jeff?"

"He stayed at the house; Mr. Debrett drove me in—he had to come to see about his car. I hope he finds they've got it ready for him."

"You mustn't let him escape without your Aunt Maggie getting a glimpse of him, you know; she's very much excited—she surprised me very much; I didn't think she knew so much about these famous personalities. I suppose he'd be too grand to come and have a little dinner with us before he goes?"

"Why too grand? Who are these film stars, anyway?"

"Well, busy people," pointed out Mr. Milward mildly. "If you can persuade him to look in, it would give your aunt pleasure. I must say that for myself, I'm a little out of touch...but Jeff says he's a fine-looking fellow."

"He's got a straight nose and a good opinion of himself—and here he comes."

The car stopped and Robert got out. It took him, Lucille noted, exactly twelve seconds to find out that golf was the passion of the old man's life, and slip into the role of the keen-but-average handicap golfer. She stood by while they discussed clubs and scores and tees; she saw Mr. Milward, standing on the pavement in the sunshine, look up at the tall, handsome actor with his mild blue eyes glistening with pleasure.

"I was just saying to Lucille that if you could find time before leaving us...my wife...a little dinner...very quiet..."

Nothing would delight Robert more. To-morrow; if his car was not ready—and it didn't look like being ready—Jeff would go and fetch the four of them in the big car: Robert and Lucille, Nicholas and Roselle. Splendid, splendid...my wife... yes, yes, charming...

They drove away; Lucille had no comment to make. She had seen Uncle Bill—steady, solemn, slow old Uncle Bill— charmed as a snake was charmed. Five minutes' chat on the pavement, and he couldn't get back into the office quick enough to telephone the good news to his wife. Potent, that was the word. It was like a tablet; if you swallowed it, it worked almost instantaneously. Well, Nicholas could do almost the same damage without any star backing. Some people did it

175

for nothing, and some people commercialised it and netted a packet—that was all.

"How long will the car be?" she enquired, and hoped it sounded merely a polite enquiry.

"They couldn't tell me. No serious damage."

"Good. Doesn't your—your studio get agitated when you vanish like this?"

"They might if I were in the middle of a film. At the moment I'm in the middle of a holiday."

There was silence, but she felt that she had made her point. When they reached the house, she drove it home ruthlessly.

"Thank you for taking me in," she said. "I always feel better when I've talked to Uncle Bill. He made me telephone my fiancé."

"Oh, yes?" Robert got out and opened the door for her.

"Perhaps I ought to have thought of it last night— but I was too bewildered. He's coming here."

"Really? When does he arrive?"

"He should be here," said Lucille, "at any moment."

Chapter Twelve

Dominic left the breakfast table and went straight out of the house, across the lawn, through the paddock and so to the home of his spirit. Up and up, to revisit his tree-house, to examine, to assess what the past year had done in the way of damage.

When he came down, he found Jeff coming out on to the lawn, and with a frown of anger made his report.

"Somebody went up my tree house," he informed him. Jeff looked down at his accusing countenance and arranged his features in the proper expression of concern.

"Well, now," he said. "You can rule me out; I haven't had time to go climbing up trees. And my father's too old to get up there."

"Then who?"

"Not the tenants; definitely not the tenants. They were rather big, both of them; if they tried to get up, the tree would've come down." Jeff pursed his lips and pondered. "Now you come to mention it, though, I do remember seeing a boy who—"

"I *knew* all the time!" Dominic gritted his teeth. "I bet it was that stinking Derek Arkwright. I bet it was. I told him if he ever went up there, I'd kick him. It was him, wasn't it?"

"He was much too far away for me to be sure," said Jeff, playing for safety. "It might have been any boy."

"It was him, I bet. I'll go and kick him."

"Oh, but wait now! Suppose it wasn't Derek Arkwright?"

Dominic was already setting off in the direction of the Templeby mansion; his lips were set firmly, and it was clear that he was going to kick Derek Arkwright as soon as he could get near enough. There was a slim chance that he hadn't been up the tree, but a good kick would ensure that he didn't go up it in future.

Jeff looked after him with some apprehension, and turned to find Simon beside him, looking extremely anxious.

"Hello," said Simon. "Have you seen Dominic anywhere?"

"Dominic? Yes—I think he's gone off to look for Derek Arkwright, but I don't think he'll find him, Simon— Derek will be at school. The term hasn't ended yet."

"I thought he'd be at school, too," said Simon, looking more harassed than ever, "but I asked the baker when he came this morning, and he says he isn't at school; he's been at home having chicken pox."

"Why couldn't he have chicken pox at school, like everybody else?" asked Jeff.

"'Cos his mother went and fetched him home when there was quarantine," explained Simon. "He's an awful sissy, and he's a softie too, and he'll go and sneak on Dominic if Dominic tells him not to go up in the tree house."

"Well, let him try this sneaking, and if his father and his mother come here to say anything, Nicholas will deal with them—both of them."

Simon's face relaxed in a smile, but his desire to keep his young brother out of trouble remained uppermost in his mind.

"I'll go and find him," he said.

He walked almost up to the ground of the Templeby's imposing estate, but search as he might, he saw no sign of Dominic. He turned back at last, and for the first part of the return journey, he kept to the paths by which he had come.

At the first cross-road, however, he hesitated; his footsteps slowed, dragged, and finally stopped altogether, and his eyes went to a distant point and remained fixed there.

The struggle was not a long one, but it was a sharp and exhausting one, and at the end of it he decided that it could do no harm just to skirt Mr. Hewett's land. Just skirt it...just walk along the footpath and see—what he could see. Even if he just caught a glimpse in the distance—the tip of a tail, the wind lifting a shaggy coat—it would be enough. That was all he wanted just now. It was all very well for Julia to talk as though she had got her books back for ever; she could believe, if she wanted to, that nothing would ever separate her from her things again. Dominic could do the repairs in his tree house and talk as if he would never again be away from it for so long as a year; he was young and he couldn't really understand. Julia was young too; Julia had said that if you thought about things as you wanted them to be, they often turned out that way. Perhaps she was right...but it was too much to risk. One parting was enough. He couldn't—he wouldn't go through that again. Never. Never, never. Long John was fairly settled— that was what Mr. Hewett had said. He had kept on going to the house at first—but then he had stopped. It wasn't fair to see him again and to make him believe it was for good, if it wasn't going to be for good. Dogs had just as many feelings as humans, and Long John must have suffered just as much as he had when they had to leave one another. It wouldn't be fair to let him know that they had all come back.

If he did know, would he remember? Some dogs forgot soon and some didn't—that was what Mr. Hewett had said, but he hadn't been able to say which sort Long John was. Could a dog forget in a year? He wasn't very old—he wasn't three yet. Did young dogs have better memories than old dogs?

It wouldn't hurt, anyway, to walk past. The footpath was a long, long way from the house, and even if Long John was outside, it wasn't likely that he'd be near the path. He'd be out in the fields chasing rabbits, or digging up things.

The house looked just the same. There was the Dutch barn; under it, in a cunning trench in the hay, Long John had liked to sleep, when Mr. Hewett first got him. A soft, fat little ball he'd been then, with brown eyes that had a fringe hanging over them. A wriggling, lolloping little ball...but he must be fully grown now. He was a very big dog a year ago; he couldn't have grown much bigger without turning into a St. Bernard, and that was the one thing, Mr. Hewett said, that wasn't included in his pedigree. How could—

There was something there...moving; something...there in among the trees, just near the house. A long way away, but who could mistake that banner of a tail? Who could—

He was turning this way. How far could dogs see? It was too far to be able to recognise anybody, that was one thing.

He was coming nearer. No, he had stopped, and was just looking. He probably thought it was a trespasser, but anyway, he wasn't moving any more; he was just standing.

It was time to get on. It wouldn't do to look backwards too much...he was still standing there. He was moving...he was coming...he was—

Simon's nerves could bear no more. He looked blindly in the direction of home, and began to walk quickly. After one more backward glance, he broke into a run, and ran, and ran, and ran, his heart thumping madly within him.

Another heart was beating fast. Jeff, listening to its thudding, wondered why Roselle, beside him, could not hear it too. But she appeared to notice nothing—her head was bent and she was studying the ground as they walked.

They had been walking for some time. The beech tree was not the place that Jeff would have chosen to walk round—it stood in the very middle of the lawn, in full view of several windows—but he had given up all hope of getting Roselle into a more propitious spot. She was being gentle and sweet, but she seemed to be more than a little absent-minded; she walked slowly but steadily; all he could do was walk beside her.

His voice penetrated at last through her meditations, and she turned to him.

"What did you say, Jeff?"

"I said"—Jeff cleared his throat—"I just said that it had seemed a long time. That you were away, I mean."

His normal calm and sensible manner had left him; he was a picture of gloom; his brow was furrowed and his mouth drooped. She was here beside him, and he had so much to say—but none of it would come out.

"It was a long time," he said again.

"It was a year," said Roselle.

"Yes. I—I missed you very much, Roselle."

There seemed to her to be nothing to say to that. He had not wanted her to go, and she had gone; it was sweet to come back and find that he hadn't forgotten, but she could not explain that she had not—at first—missed him. She had not missed him in the way that he had missed her. When she had wept, in London, and longed for home, she had not thought of him—at first; he had been part of the enormous ache in her heart. She had never analysed her grief; she had cried because she had wanted to be at home, and she had not—at first—specified, item by item, what she meant by home. He had always, from her earliest days, been part of it. He had lived more of his life at her house than he had at his own; he had always appeared on the first day of the holidays and disappeared on the last day. He had been nobody's special friend—at first. Then he had gone into his father's office and she had grown older; he had begun to visit the house to see, not the others, but herself. She had never known Wood Mount without him, and that was why she could not reply and tell him that she had missed him, because it would have meant explaining that she thought of him as part of her home, part of her background, part of everything she loved.

"Roselle—"

"Yes, Jeff?"

"Lucille said you weren't going back to London. She said you'd given up your job for good. Is that so?"

"Yes."

She hoped that he would not ask her why. She found evasion difficult and lying impossible; if he asked her her reasons for leaving London, she would have to tell him that nothing had been as she had imagined, and that in imagining it at all, she had shown herself to be more childish, more foolish than she cared to have him think her. She would like him to accept the fact of her return and not to enquire into its causes.

Jeff was not thinking about why she had come home; he was only wondering what she meant to do next. It was not much use asking her, because whatever she did must depend on Lucille and Nicholas. Nicholas was going to do his best to keep the house—but if Lucille didn't agree— if Roselle went away again—it hardly bore thinking of.

Jeff's heart slid slowly down and rested on his brogues—perhaps they would persuade her to go to Cornwall. She might go away again to live near Lucille—and this time, perhaps, she would stay away for ever. Unless...unless he laced up his courage and told her what she meant to him.

"Roselle—I do hope you can stay here."

"In this house? Lucille says we can't."

"If not in this house, then in Greenhurst. My mother would be very happy to have you for as long as you cared to stay. She—you know she loves you, Roselle."

"Yes. Thank you, Jeff."

She was looking at him, and there was a look in her blue eyes that made Jeff's heart rise slowly to its own site once more. She had never looked like this before—never, never, so soft and so sweet and so—Jeff found the term at last—so yielding. He put out a hand and took one of hers, and they did a complete circle round the tree without speaking. Words rushed to his lips and were choked back again; he longed to speak, but what, he asked himself dismally, what was the use? He had opened his mouth too wide already, and he was a cad, a brute, a low-down philanderer who hadn't the right to lick Roselle's boots, even if she wore boots. He was weak-kneed and faithless, and he ought to be cut into small pieces and thrown to the dogs. He had betrayed Roselle. He had forfeited her love.

He had kissed Miriam Arkwright.

He had kissed her. Worse, he had spoken wild words of love. He wished he could remember exactly what words they had been—but he had been drinking champagne, and champagne always had that effect on him. It wasn't the champagne; it was the thought of drinking it—that, and the opulent look of the Templeby mansion behind him as he stood on the terrace with Miriam. And perhaps there had been, too, the comfortable feeling that a man like himself, a man with not a drop of blue blood in his veins and not too much credit in his Bank account, could whisper in the ears of a Templeby maiden without too much fear of consequences. The assumption, he now saw, had been an entirely erroneous one; ever since that evening, Miriam Arkwright had sought him out in what even his mother felt to be a proprietary manner. But he had never done more than whisper, and he had never—almost never— forgotten Roselle. And Roselle was here now, and he loved her and if he didn't tell her so, openly and without equivocation, she would go away again, and be lost to him.

The thought stabbed him into action. Taking a firmer grasp of Roselle's hand, he led her into the shelter of the rhododendrons; here they would be unobserved. Nobody looking out of the windows could see them. He reached the thickest bush and stopped, and Roselle stood beside him and realised, with a shaking wave of emotion in which gratitude was predominant, that she need never go away from Greenhurst again. He loved her; he had loved her throughout the year they had been parted, while she— she had thought of him only as part of her home. Until her return, until she had seen him again, she had not known what he really meant to her. He had thought only of her; she had been selfishly absorbed in her own dreams. He was patient and loyal and strong, and she knew—at last—that she loved him.

"Roselle—"

"Yes, Jeff?"

"I love you, Roselle. I love you very much. Do you— could you love me—a little?"

"Yes, Jeff. I could. I mean—I do."

It was undoubtedly the most concise contract ever drawn up, but, enfolded in one another's arms, neither of them had any thought but that of relief. It was over; they were together. With Roselle held thus in his arms, Jeff felt that he could face all the Templebys who had ever been heard of, from the Field of the Cloth of Gold onwards. His conscience was clear.

Further, his brain was working. Lucille's problem, which he had regarded, up to now, as a, purely family matter, had now come to be one which concerned him closely. He was no longer a sympathetic spectator; he was allied to them, one of them. They were to be his relations; he would even be responsible, in a measure, for the welfare of the younger members.

An idea began to form; it was too early to decide whether it was a good or bad idea, but he could put it to Nicholas— if

Roselle agreed. It was worth a try...

"Roselle—"

"Yes, Jeff?"

"Listen..."

And as Roselle listened, a large and opulent looking car drove up and the door bell gave a peremptory clang.

Pietro answered it, and Lady Templeby looked at him in surprise. She had not troubled to call on the late tenants of the house, but she had kept herself informed of their circumstances and their staff. Nobody had mentioned a brigand. She exchanged a glance with her daughter, who stood beside her.

"Is Miss Wayne at home?" she enquired.

Pietro bowed them in and led the way to the drawing room. Finding it empty, he turned and put a hand on Lady Templeby's out-thrust bosom and halted her as she was following him into the room.

Nobody," he told her. "Come here, please."

Benumbed, they followed him to the study. Miss Cornhill was sitting on the sofa mending Julia's coat. As Pietro ushered the visitors in, flashed a smile and withdrew, she rose to point out that there had been a mistake—but Lady Templeby was in, and had her own reasons for staying in.

"I am Lady Templeby and this is my daughter, Miss Arkwright," she said. "I would like to speak to Miss Wayne."

There was a second's pause; some sort of mother's help, decided Lady Templeby. Titled, thought Miss Cornhill, but no

True Breeding.

"I am sorry," she said. "Miss Wayne is out—and so is Mr. Wayne."

"I don't think I know your name," said Lady Templeby.

"I am Miss Cornhill, and I am here," improvised Miss Cornhill, to her own amazement, "as a temporary housekeeper."

"I see." Lady Templeby seated herself and signed to her daughter to do the same. "This is not, in a strict sense, a social call," she said. "I have come on a somewhat grave matter concerning Dominic Wayne who, I understand, came home yesterday."

Miss Cornhill waited formidably; she was resolved not to speak to this disagreeable woman more than was necessary.

"I've come on a matter which I think ought to be looked into at once," went on Lady Templeby.

"Miss Wayne will be away all the morning, I'm afraid. Perhaps some other time—"

"It's an extremely serious matter. I brought my daughter with me because it was she who actually witnessed the attack."

"Attack?" Miss Cornhill showed her first sign of interest. "What attack?"

"There is no other word for it. It was an attack— savage and unprovoked. I have always said that Dominic Wayne wanted really firm handling, and this proves it. I've always maintained that—"

"Whom did he attack?" asked Miss Cornhill.

"He waited for my son—he actually, I think, lay in wait for him, and then he...he *kicked* him! My daughter saw the whole thing. He kicked him on the shins—twice. It was the act of a young bully. A ruffian."

Miss Cornhill was silent, struggling with unfamiliar and conflicting feelings. It was wrong to kick Lady Templeby's little boy—but if he was anything like his mother and that sour-looking daughter, how right, how very right that he should be kicked! But how wrong, how very wrong that she, Vera Cornhill, should think so. What had come over her?

This was not the time to find out; Lady Templeby was plunging angrily on.

"Derek is older than Dominic, so there could be no question of retaliation. Furthermore, he has been brought up not to use violence of any kind, especially towards those younger than himself. He took the sensible course of running at once to summon me—but by the time I got to the scene, Dominic had, of course, made off. It was a most savage attack, wasn't it, Miriam?"

"Mm? Oh yes, it was." Miriam, with an effort, withdrew her gaze from the pale gleam to be seen through the rhododendrons. She was certain they were out there. Jeff Milward was not in Greenhurst—they had enquired at the Office on the way here. He was not in Greenhurst— and Roselle Wayne was home again...and anything might happen. It was a mean trick for Fate to have played on a girl. Ever since the night of the dance, Jeff had been as good as hers, and it wasn't fair that Roselle should come back and snatch him away. It was a mean, low trick—the kind that Fate was always serving her....

Miss Cornhill, following her glance, saw the distant blur of Roselle's dress, and without hesitation emptied her basket of cotton reels on to Miss Arkwright's lap.

"Oh—how clumsy of me!" She helped Miriam to replace them in the basket, and by the time the task was done, saw with deep satisfaction that Jeff and Roselle had walked out of view. Miss Cornhill, dizzy with the realisation of how deeply she had involved herself in the affairs of the Waynes, made no attempt to return to her seat; instead, she addressed Lady Templeby formally.

"I will tell Miss Wayne about this when she returns," she said.

"I hope something will be done."

"Certainly."

"I hope you agree that it was entirely uncalled for."

"Certainly."

"Those children have never had any proper parental control; all children need discipline."

"Certainly."

"I hope you will see that the matter is dealt with at once."

"Certainly." Why didn't the woman go?

Lady Templeby was peering out of the window with narrowed eyes.

"Is Mr. Milward here? There are one or two things I would like to see him about and—"

"He came out," said Miss Cornhill, "to drive Miss Wayne into town."

And that was the truth.

Baffled, Lady Templeby went away, taking her daughter with her. Miss Cornhill accompanied them to the front door and, closing it behind them, went upstairs slowly and shut herself into her bedroom to think.

Twenty-four hours...less. This time yesterday, she had been minding her own business and leading an orderly and leisured existence. To-day...

To-day, she was here.

And she was...the sensation was so extraordinary, so rare, that she had to be quite sure before she put a name to it, labelled it. But facts were facts, and she had been taught to face them, pleasant or unpleasant—and this one was very pleasant.

She was enjoying herself.

There was so much to be done here. On all sides, she could see work that waited to be done. This house—the house itself—was beautiful, but since their arrival last night, it had been far from orderly. Work—it cried out to be done. Tidying, dusting, sewing, and then more dusting and tidying. She had not spent years as a school Matron without being aware of the dirt and the damage that accompanied small boys wherever they went. She had retired; she had a competence; she could live in her little room at the boarding house, safe, snug, until she died. That was what she had worked for and that was what she had earned. A quiet backwater—peace—serenity. And, now she had been hurled among the Waynes—without money, without her possessions. Nicholas was at this moment instituting enquiries at the station; her luggage would be found and returned to her; she would be free to go.

And Miss Cornhill, staring out of the study window at the now plainly-visible forms of Jeff and Roselle, knew that she had no desire to go.

She was still staring out of the window when she heard the car, and the voices of Lucille and Robert Debrett. Shortly afterwards there came the splutter of Nicholas's motor-bike. Miss Cornhill walked into the hall, but after a glance at her watch saw that this was not the time to introduce the subject of Dominic and the kick on the shins; it was time for lunch.

When they were assembled, there was no sign of Simon.

"He went looking for Dominic—but that was a long time ago," said Jeff.

"He's back: I saw him," said Julia. "I was up in the attic, sorting books, and I saw him."

"Well, he'll turn up," said Nicholas.

Robert Debrett was at the door, and he prepared to shut it. As he did so, a movement outside caught his eye, and he saw Simon disappearing into the pantry at the end of the corridor.

"I think he's here now," he said.

He went out and Lucille followed him; together they walked along the corridor, and as they reached the pantry door, Lucille made to pass him, but with a swift movement, he put out a hand and stopped her. She looked past him into the room and then stood silent.

Simon was standing by the table in the middle of the room, staring through the window at the empty square of garden outside. Lucille saw that he was panting and, although their arrival had not been accomplished without noise, he was unaware of their presence at the door.

She was about to speak when something in his tense attitude made her pause. He was waiting for something— but what could come through the pantry window? What could— but of course! This was the window through which Long John had always come. This was the window which had been left open always, for the comings and goings of a restless puppy; there were old scratches on the window sill, and the plants growing beneath the window had always been in a sorry state, battered and trampled by his huge paws.

The window was closed now, but as they stood, unmoving, there was a sound outside. Something—something heavy, seemed to have dropped on to the flower beds that the tenants had carefully restored. Something was to be heard...and now it was to be seen. Two enormous paws and a head—a huge, shaggy head and a pair of brown eyes peering out of their almost obscuring fringe.

There was a second's pause. Lucille looked at Simon and

saw that he was unable to move.

Somebody had better move, she decided, before the dog had broken his way through. He was uttering loud, triumphant yelps, and his paws were drumming, scratching, tearing at the window panes.

She walked forward and unlatched the window. Before it had opened more than a foot, a hairy body had launched itself past her, over a chair, and on to the waiting boy. There was a thump as the two hit the ground together, and then boy and dog were inextricably mixed up and a hysterical tail, two groping hands, a brown smooth head and a black and white shaggy one appeared and vanished and appeared again. The dog's yelps were joined by other, quieter, murmuring sounds as Simon talked in the language that Long John knew so well. His eyes were shining; on his cheeks stood the tears he so rarely shed.

Lucille stood looking down at them for some time, and her face was expressionless. Soon she would have to look up and meet Robert Debrett's eyes and the accusation in them.

But when she looked up at last, Robert was not looking at her. His gaze was on Simon, and Lucille, after hesitating for a moment, went out of the room and left the three of them together.

Chapter Thirteen

If Digby Russell had been twenty-five instead of thirty-five; if Lucille, when telephoning to him, had been less anxious to appear calm and in command of the situation; above all, if she had let fall a hint that filmland's most eligible bachelor was a guest in her house, her fiancé would, possibly, have put down the receiver and gone out to his car and driven straight and swiftly to Wood Mount.

His first impulse, indeed, had been to leave at once, but as he gave his attention once more to his work and saw the expression of disapproval on the face of his clerk when he spoke of his imminent departure, he began to feel that perhaps the sound of Lucille's voice, sounding so unexpectedly, so warmly in his ear, was making him act too hastily. The matter was not, after all, so urgent; he could tidy up affairs here in the office, and leave for Hampshire the next day.

His mother, to whom he communicated his decision that evening, seemed to feel that even this plan was somewhat hasty. It did not greatly matter, she pointed out, whether he got to Wood Mount now, or in two or three days; if the house had been sold and the new owners had been chafing to get in, it would have been different; as it was, a day or two could not make any difference; moreover, it would be the week-end, so that his absence would not interfere with his work. This head-long behaviour on the part of Lucille's family indicated, didn't he think, something bordering on the uncontrolled? Digby said that it did, rather. It sounded, went on his mother, as though the younger children were really rather out of hand. Digby said that it did, rather. It would be well, concluded his mother, to draw up a plan before he went; Lucille was charming, but not perhaps quite up to handling all those unruly elements; it would be better to have some scheme to propose to her.

Digby said that it would, rather, and communicated his change of plan to Lucille in a telephone call that evening. She heard him out without comment, and then returned to the drawing-room, where the household was assembled. Nicholas looked up from the hearthrug, on which he was sprawled playing draughts with Julia.

"Who was it?"

"Digby."

Robert, playing Beggar My Neighbour with Dominic, gave no sign of interest beyond putting down two plain cards for a King, instead of three, and then sweeping the trick absently and illegally into his own pile.

"Hey, that was mine!" protested Dominic.

"It was? So it was—and I owe you one more. Next thing you know, I'll be cheating purposely. Tck tck tck. Here you are."

Digby was delayed, was he? Good. That meant he could hang on here a bit longer. Once Digby walked in, he meant to walk out; Robert was well aware that he would not be looked upon with favour by Mr. Russell. But now he was delayed, and so this nice cosy family life could go on for a little longer.

Lucille looked round the room and the same adjectives sprang to her mind. Nothing, she thought, could look more ideally domestic than this gathering. Miss Cornhill, there on a window seat, sewing something of Dominic's and looking as though she had been in the family for generations; Pietro drawing a map of Italy for Simon, as they both lay on their stomachs on the floor. The entire group looked placid, pleased and—permanent. It was fantastic, but there it was. They should all be somewhere else—but here they all were. Digby's conversation on the telephone echoed with a mocking and hollow sound—try to manage, he had said; he would be here as soon as he reasonably could. If the situation got out of hand, he would of course, set off at once—but there were one or two things—it was difficult, rather.

There were no difficulties here, she mused. The house was running like a dream. Miss Cornhill was to all intents and purposes running the place—and Pietro was performing marvels in the kitchen, even without ducks and red wine. If only Nicholas had brought a gardener with him when he returned, they could have put up a notice: Vacancies filled. There was even the dog. They were—one would have said, looking at them now—a right little, tight little family. Except for that big,

197

handsome deb's dream sitting there doing a children-adore-me act.

It might be an act, she reflected, but the children did like him. Simon's large, serious eyes followed him wherever he went; Dominic had admitted him to his tree house—and for a man who seemed to take so little exercise, Robert Debrett had got up the tree with remarkable skill and swiftness. He and Nicholas...brothers, no less.

The thought came to her suddenly that it was unfair to expect Digby to stand up to this competition. There was nothing the matter with Digby; if the children had seen him first, they would have...they might have liked him. One didn't, as she knew from her own experience, appreciate his good qualities at a first meeting—but once they got used to him...she rejected the term, seeking one more loyal. To have to present him to the children—even to Roselle and Nicholas—with their eyes, their minds, full of Robert Debrett—it was unfair, and it was going to make things very much more difficult.

This Debrett...after twenty-four hours they were all—except herself—treating him as one of the family; Nicholas was asking his advice; worse, he was taking it. Miss Cornhill was consulting him, Pietro was providing exotic dishes which only the two of them had ever heard of.

Robert looked up for a moment from the cards and met her gaze, and he saw with some surprise that the expression in her eyes was less openly antagonistic than it had been since his arrival. He went back to his game, speculating quietly on the reason for this.

Lucille, indeed, was feeling that she had done him less than justice. It was not his fault that he was a famous and sought-after figure; it was not his fault that he had roused in her irritation and a feeling that he was using this interlude to indulge a liking for family life. He hadn't sought them out; he had performed a kindness and in doing so had come among them. If she thought he was staying too long, certainly nobody else did, and as he had made it clear, without saying anything, that he would go immediately Digby came, perhaps she had been giving him less than his due.

Her thoughts went to Roselle and Jeff; they were out, nobody knew where. Jeff had said nothing to her about his feelings, but it was quite obvious that the family was going to have yet another member added to it. She had been wrong in this matter, and Nicholas had been right—and an engagement between Jeff and Roselle would give him a firmer basis for his proposition of keeping on the house.

Wood Mount...she was to leave it, but not to strangers, which would have been comparatively easy. She was to go away and leave everything, everybody she loved here in this house. Everybody, that is, but Digby. She was to live in Cornwall, in the Russell's great, ugly, echoing house; Mrs. Russell would have her own rooms, but they were to eat together. Digby's mother...for breakfast, for lunch, for tea, for dinner every day. The long, thin face, just like Digby's; the quiet, flat voice and the even flatter statements. Large rooms, quiet rooms; yes, certainly quiet; there would be nothing of the hurly-burly in which she had lived and moved all her life. One couldn't, of course, take one's childhood, one's girlhood into marriage. Husbands were like magnets—you got drawn in and sucked up and there you were, attached; stuck. Wherever he went, you went, even unto what used to be called the Outposts of Empire. Your old life was left behind and you set forth with your mate.

Mate—Digby.

Digby—Mate.

It didn't go, somehow. And she felt sure that he would not care to be referred to as a mate; there was something earthy, even coarse about the term that wouldn't, she knew, appeal to him. He would be a tender lover, perhaps; a reliable, a good, a fine husband, probably; but mate? Perhaps not.

Certainly not.

Definitely not.

She was roused by the extraordinary, the fantastic and at the same time quite real picture of Miss Cornhill shepherding the younger members of the family to bed. Pietro went to the kitchen to concoct the preliminaries of to-morrow's special dish. Robert uncoiled himself from the floor and leaned out of the window to look at the lovely night.

"Stars, millions and millions," he said, without turning. "Nicholas, would your sister trust herself with me out there under them?"

"Surely," said Nicholas. "She's armed against ı. strangers—she's got this Digby chap, remember?"

"If I don't remember, I feel she'll remind me." Robeı. turned to look at Lucille. "How about it?" he asked. "It's a wonderful night for love."

"Go on, Lu," urged Nicholas. "If he gets above himself, give our old call whistle—remember it?"

He pursed his lips and gave vent to a shrill, melodious theme; from upstairs, on the instant, came the children's responses; the same notes, the same signal.

"There you are," smiled Nicholas. "Or have you forgotten how to whistle?"

Lucille said nothing, because—suddenly—she could not speak. The call was one which went further back than their own childhood; their father had used it, and his father. It was a small thing—a special family whistle, useful sometimes to locate one another in crowds, on expeditions; a special call to special people. But she had not used it for over a year—and in the life to which she was going, there would be no whistling. Whistling was out.

She stood up, leaving a remark over her shoulder as she went out of the room.

"I'll get a coat," she said.

She walked with Robert through the paddock and along the path through the fields beyond. The air was cool and clear, and Lucille, with a sudden feeling of enjoyment in the exercise, quickened her step and found Robert lengthening his stride.

"There's a nice walk down to an old mill, and back another way," she told him. "It'll take about an hour, if you want a real walk."

They went, at first, in silence; then she began to ask him about his work, and found herself learning something about his life. She put aside, for the moment, all the reservations she had felt about him, and gave herself up wholly and deliberately to an enjoyment of his company. There was everything here that a woman could want, a quiet peaceful scene beneath the stars, a man, tall and broad, by her side, talking in a voice trained for this very purpose— to beguile his listeners and make them forget everything but what he was saying.

Walking in the starlight with Robert Debrett. A slow smile curved Lucille's lips. She had seen him doing this on the screen—and now he was here beside her, giving her a benefit performance. For free. They said that red-heads were hotheads; this was a time when she could be thankful that her head was cool, and that she could use it to remember how often he must have done this in the past—not always before the cameras, but always with a markedly professional finish.

She wondered fleetingly what Digby would say if he could see her now. He would be upset, rather.

In the meantime, she was enjoying herself very much. It was impossible to know whether Robert Debrett was enjoying it too, but she decided that that wasn't important; he was being kind, and she was grateful.

They stopped at the mill and looked up at the ruined shell silhouetted against the sky.

"We used to swim here," Lucille told him. "It was cold, but it was fun. Nicholas nearly drowned once—fooling about."

"He's a nice fellow," said Robert, "and if it doesn't sound too presumptuous from a comparative stranger, I think his idea of keeping the house is a good one. Are you going to let him do it?"

"I don't suppose letting him will come into it," said Lucille. "It's almost twenty-four hours since I was the head of the family. Now I'm just hovering on the edge of things, watching them all."

"It must be good to know that things will go on satisfactorily when you've gone away; it must make you feel better."

"Well, it doesn't make me feel better; it just makes me feel lonely. I suppose I've got so used to ordering them about that I don't take kindly to the idea of...just stepping out. That's what Uncle Bill said, anyway."

"How long have you known your fiancé?" he asked, as they walked on.

"Digby? Seven—eight months."

"He's round about thirty, isn't he?"

"Thirty-five. He doesn't look it; he's the type that doesn't age much. Slim and boyish; in twenty years he'll probably still look slim and boyish and I'll look like his mother, instead of like his wife."

"Twenty years...Marriage is a long contract," he mused. "I suppose it doesn't seem long when the Lucilles and the Nicholases and the Roselles start appearing. I think it's a good idea, this one of your parents—having a family in two separate halves."

"No, it isn't a good idea. Just when my parents were beginning to relax, they had to go back to the beginning and bring up Simon and the other two. It's a bad idea—it's bad for the second lot of children, too, in a way. They don't get the same interest and attention that the first lot did—at least, that's the way it was with us. You have to be tough to cope with a large family—you have to keep at them. My parents weren't young enough; they couldn't stand up to it when things like staff and money became difficult. Were your parents young?"

"My mother was; my father was twenty-four years older than she was—but it worked out very well. As a matter of fact, she died before he did."

"Were you famous before they died?"

He laughed.

"No. I was in a small repertory company doing odd parts and painting scenery in my spare time. It wasn't until I was cast as Bassanio in the *Merchant* film that I got going. I looked fine in those tights—and of course, the part's what Julia would call a pet of a one."

He talked no more about himself; he went on to speak of Julia, and Simon and Dominic; from Dominic, they got somehow to Denmark and from there to Europe and travel, and

Robert learned the story of the old lady who was to have taken Lucille to the cities of her dreams...and who had remained at home.

The shape of Wood Mount appeared before them, and Lucille sighed a little to herself. It was over—but it had been a pleasant hour from which in some strange way she had derived strength and comfort. Perhaps the incident would emerge, in later years, as one of those wistful, faintly embarrassing little romantic episodes her mother had sometimes related to her. She could tell her children about the walk, and touch up the details with a little glamour and romance. She need not explain that he had taken her hand firmly into his, at the end, in a merely friendly, brotherly way; she could say he took it—and leave it at that.

As they reached the house, Roselle came down the steps to meet them. It was too dark to see her expression, but her excitement could be plainly felt.

"Oh...Lucille. We...we were looking for you."

"Well, here I am."

"Jeff's inside, talking to Nicholas."

"Well, come on in, then."

"N-no. No, I think I'll stay here—but you go in. Jeff wants to see you."

Robert's laugh came through the darkness, and Roselle's echoed it a little shakily.

"Where do you keep the champagne, Lucille?" he asked.

"In the shop. Roselle, are you—"

"Of course she is," said Robert. "Roselle, can I give you a kiss of pure—quite pure congratulation?"

"Oh, please! Robert, isn't it...wonderful?"

"He's a lucky man." Robert put out a hand as Lucille moved toward the steps. "No, don't go," he said. "Let him get Nicholas's blessing and then you can go in and give him yours."

In the drawing-room with Nicholas, Jeff said his piece.

"I wasn't sure," he ended, "whether to talk to Lucille, or whether you were the head of the house. The suitor ought to go to Papa, as far as I know.

"You can look on me as Papa," said Nicholas, "and you can have Roselle and welcome—but there's one small item: if rumour isn't lying, you've already got a girl fastened round your neck."

"I'm a free man," declared Jeff stoutly. "My conscience is absolutely clear."

"Who's talking about your conscience? I'm talking about your commitments. That Templeby crowd won't take this lying down."

"There was nothing in it; nothing at all."

"I hope they agree with you."

"Look," said Jeff irritably, "this is the greatest moment of my life, and you stand there casting slurs. Do I marry Roselle with your co-operation or without it?"

"You don't need my co-operation," said Nicholas, "but I do need yours. Did your father tell you I'm planning to take over the house?"

"Yes. I think it's a sound idea, and if you're going on to say that Roselle and I can come and live here, that's fine; I'd thought of it myself, and put it to Roselle, and she's all for it. But do you look after the younger ones, or do we?"

"Don't hurry me into anything, but I think I can make a deal with this Cornhill to stay on and keep the three of them in order."

"What'll you give her for money?"

"Don't hurry me," repeated Nicholas. "But we'd be mad not to recognise luck when it blew right into our faces like this, Jeff; there's Miss Cornhill falling more deeply under our spell every hour, and there's that Italian comedian who's—"

"I think he's got his eye on a job with Robert."

"Well, we can tip Robert off and say we want him ourselves."

"And what'll you—"

"Give him for money? My God, you do harp, don't you? For all you know, they might both offer to pay us for staying on here and working for us. Now let's forget it and go and kiss Roselle, you and me both. And then I'll bring down my trumpet and play to you."

"Don't you bother; we'll—"

"And play to you," repeated Nicholas firmly. "Now come on."

207

Chapter Fourteen

There was no news of Digby the next day; there was no letter in the morning, and no telephone call in the evening. Nobody noticed the omission except Lucille—and Robert Debrett, and neither of them was disposed to comment upon it.

Robert went into Greenhurst during the afternoon, and returned in his car; when they were ready to set out to the Milwards for dinner, Robert sat in front besides Nicholas, who wanted to handle a Rolls for the first and probably, he added, the only time; Lucille and Roselle sat behind.

The dinner was in the nature of a celebration; there were toasts to Roselle's future, to Lucille's future, even to Robert's future which seemed, said Mr. Milward, with unwonted humour, already reasonably secure. The women helped to dish up, the men helped to wash up—but when they had settled down afterwards in the little drawing-room, the party was interrupted by a telephone call from Julia. A man had come, she said.

"You mean Digby?" said Jeff, who had answered the telephone.

"I don't know. I suppose so. Pietro let him in and he just said he wanted to see Miss Wayne, and Pietro took him into the drawing-room, and told Miss Cornhill, and Miss Cornhill came and told me, and said she thought I'd better see him, so I came down in my pyjamas to telephone and tell somebody about him."

"But haven't you seen him?"

"I saw him from the bedroom window when he came. I heard his car and I thought it was Robert coming back and I looked out, but it wasn't Robert—it was a taxi, and it went away and left a sort of thin man with glasses. If that's Digby, I think he looks a bit gruesome."

Jeff remembered that the telephone was on the hall table, just outside the door of the drawing-room. He also remembered the carrying quality of Julia's voice.

"Don't talk so loud; he'll hear you," he warned.

"No, he can't hear—he's shut in the drawing-room. Shall I tell him to go away and come back to-morrow?"

"No, don't be an ass, Julia; you can't do that. I'll tell Lucille...look, I'll call her. It may not be Digby."

"I bet it is. He looks just like a Digby. I said he would, didn't I."

"Look, shut-up, Julia, or he'll hear you. I'll put Lucille on, and you go on in and ask him to come to the phone."

"In my pyjamas?"

"Haven't you got a dressing-gown, for pete's sake?"

"No; my luggage hasn't come from school yet. These are Nicholas's pyjamas."

"Well, never mind whose pyjamas they are; you go and call Digby—I'm going to fetch Lucille."

Lucille returned to the drawing-room to announce that her fiancé had arrived by train, and was waiting for her at Wood Mount. Robert was the first to break the silence that followed.

"I'll drive you back," he said.

"No, I'll take her," said Nicholas. "Or no—perhaps you'd better; then you can leave Lucille with him and come back here, and we needn't break up the party."

"All right," agreed Robert.

They began to drive to Wood Mount, and Lucille sat silent, hoping she was not looking as angry as she felt. Digby could at least have telephoned that he was on his way; he could have sent a wire to say that he was coming. To appear at this time of the evening...

It was not, she had to acknowledge, late. If they had been at home, they would just have finished dinner; Digby, with his usual consideration, would have had his dinner on the way, and his arrival was no doubt timed with the idea of getting an opportunity to talk to her after the children had gone to bed. There was nothing to blame him for, but Lucille—squaring up to the fact with all the honesty of her nature—knew that his coming had put an end to a peaceful, even a magical interlude. From now on, arguments would begin—and whatever happened at the end, she herself would be going away from Wood Mount for ever.

And long before that...to-morrow, perhaps...Robert Debrett would also be going away—for ever.

The thought left her with a cold feeling which she thought it unwise to analyse. It would be madness to try to sort out the confused impressions of the last two days; all she had to do now...was put the whole thing into Digby's hands and watch him straightening out the tangle.

They spoke scarcely a word on the way home, but Lucille got out of the car with the curious feeling that a great deal had been said. Robert helped her out and watched her as she went up the steps.

"Good luck," he called softly.

She looked back at him and tried to speak. No words came, however, and she merely raised a hand and then went into the house.

The picture that met her eyes in the drawing-room was not an encouraging one. Digby was sitting on the edge of a chair on one side of the fireplace; in a chair opposite sat Julia, cross-legged, pyjama-clad, with an expression on her face that spoke only too clearly of utter and abysmal boredom. Digby, glassy-eyed, was still doing his best, but his relief, his almost joyous bound from his chair as Lucille appeared, came as near to enthusiasm as she had ever seen him display.

"Ah—Lucille, my dear."

"I think I'll go to bed now," said Julia, rising with a huge yawn. "I was talking to him till you came, Lu."

It was plain that she felt this act merited all Lucille's gratitude. As she went out and closed the door, Digby's lips parted in a stifled sigh of relief. If they were all like that...! And he had done his best. He had ignored the remarks overheard on the telephone; he had treated her as one should always, he had heard, treat children—as though they were grown up. He had talked of every subject in the world calculated to hold the interest of a ten-year-old—and she had sat there looking at him as though he had been something on a slide; unwinking, wondering, and plainly bored.

He took Lucille in his arms and kissed her gently.

"I came as soon as I could," he said. "How is everything?"

"Working out," said Lucille. "Did anybody offer you a drink, Digby?"

"No; I don't want one, thank you. I hope you've room for me; Julia seemed to indicate that the house was full."

"Your room's ready. I'm sorry I wasn't here when you arrived—we were asked to dinner at Uncle Bill's."

"Uncle Bill...ah, Mr. Milward," said Digby, pleased to be able to show his grasp of the cast. "I expect I shall be meeting him to-morrow. Has anything at all been settled, Lucille?"

He was certainly a conscientious man, she reflected, looking at him with a gaze that she fought to keep from becoming too keen, too analytic. He had come to discuss this matter, and here he was, discussing it.

"Let's leave it till to-morrow, Digby," she said. "I'm rather tired to-night."

"As you like, of course. But as we're alone..."

'Now we're alone, it's high time we were making love...' The words of the currently popular song, the tune of which Nicholas played a dozen times a day, came to Lucille's mind. But that sort of song—like whistling— would not go down well with the Russells. Digby and his mother called themselves musical and went to a great many concerts, but they would not enjoy *'Now we're alone'*.

"Let's go up and I'll show you where I've put you; it isn't the room I wanted you to have," she said, as they went up the stairs, "but things have been rather confused lately."

"The foreign-looking man who let me in—"

He paused. Pietro had appeared on the landing, clad in a pair of Robert's pyjamas and a dressing-gown that had once belonged to Lucille's father. He was on his way downstairs to look at the boiler, an invention he was convinced was designed especially to plague him.

"Ah. The lover!" he cried. "I tell Mees Cornhill, and she say 'No, that cannot be'—but I was right, so, Signor, you are a very lucky man; very lucky. You have a beautiful wife; she will have beautiful children. Men will be at her feet; they will adore her. You too, adore her, no?"

"Well, yes, I do, rather," said Digby, endeavouring to edge

past the speaker.

"I will not keep you; she is taking you to your bedroom. Soon"—Pietro gave a leer that made Digby's scalp crawl— "soon it will be the other way about, no? I give you both my salutations; you will be so happy, so happy, so happy!"

At the third repetition, Pietro was well on his way downstairs. Digby looked at Lucille, and she saw that his face was pale.

"My word!" he murmured. "Very foreign."

"In here," said Lucille, opening a door. "Will you be comfortable?"

"Thank you—yes, of course. This is a beautiful house," he commented. "I can understand why you hesitated before parting with it."

She paused on her way out, looked at him for a moment, and then decided that she would take it up in the morning.

"Good-night, Digby."

"Good-night, my dear." He came over and kissed her, and she put her hands on his shoulders and looked at him earnestly.

"I've got a nice family," she said slowly, "but you might find them difficult to get to know."

"I've got a long time to do it in," he reminded her. "The rest of my life."

"You may need it."

"Who's this Debrett fellow that appears to have rescued Simon? Not the actor, is he? Julia must have got it wrong."

"No, she got it right."

"My word, you must have your hands full with them all."

Not the jealous type, Digby, she reflected, shutting the door and going downstairs again. He thought she was going to bed, but she wasn't going to bed yet. For two pins, she thought rebelliously, she would go back to the party. They had all been happy, they had all been enjoying themselves...it was mean to think that Digby had put a damper on everything, but he did have a way of reducing things to a sensible level. She ought to be thankful that he was so level-headed, but...

She was in the kitchen when the others returned, sitting at the table with Pietro, and cutting sandwiches for them all. Nicholas looked in and then ushered in Robert and Roselle.

"Where's Digby?" he asked in surprise.

"In bed. He was...he was tired...and there was no point in his waiting up."

"None—unless he wanted to meet Roselle—and me," observed Nicholas dryly. "Food; good. Tuck in, fellows."

Lucille made coffee, and they all sat round drinking it.

It was long past midnight, and she ought not to have waited up for their return, but she felt happy—and strangely relieved. Digby had come, and perhaps it wasn't going to be such an upheaval after all.

Roselle was the first to go upstairs to bed; Pietro was next, but he went only because Nicholas led him to the door and forcibly ejected him; he had got only half way through his life

215

story, recounted with all the picturesque details that he had left out in previous recitals; there was a great deal more, and he would dearly have liked to stay and tell them about it.

"To-morrow," said Nicholas firmly. "I'll put a marker in page four thousand two hundred and eighty—and we'll read on from there. Now go on." He shut the door on him and yawned widely. "Ah-oh! I'm off. You coming, Robert?"

"Not yet. There's more coffee here."

"Well, I'm going. Good night, Robert; good night, Lucille."

He went out, and Robert looked across the table at Lucille.

"Well, what did he say?" he enquired. "Did he have any suggestions?"

"Heaps, but we left them until the morning."

"I'm looking forward to meeting him. He must be an extraordinary man."

She looked at him a little warily.

"Why?"

"Because if I'd come a long way to see you, and found you alone, I wouldn't have gone to bed...alone," he said deliberately.

"I don't suppose you would." Lucille's voice was suddenly cold. "You'd probably have done what you wanted to do, instead of what somebody else wanted you to do."

"Hard words—but no doubt true," he acknowledged. "But

he must be the bloodless type."

"He is. He wouldn't make one of those smouldering screen lovers. But he's got some qualities almost as good—decency and kindness, for example. The fact that we weren't in a huddle on the sofa when you came in might seem odd to you, but we don't all have your technique and experience. And the fact that he can go placidly to bed and leave his future wife alone with you doesn't mean that he's underestimating your charms; it simply means that he—"

"—underestimates yours," put in Robert, and saw her rising to her feet.

"The coffee's behind you," she said, "and if you're still hungry, there's bread and butter there, and the rest of the ham."

"If I promised to keep my mouth shut, would you stay?"

"No. I'm tired. Good night."

"You're angry with me, aren't you?"

"No. I'm tired, I told you."

He was between her and the door; he did not look as though he were deliberately barring her way, but she hesitated for a moment.

He looked at her, but he knew, suddenly, that he could say and do nothing that would help him to an understanding with her. His name and his fame had put a barrier between them, a barrier she had erected to defend herself against any assumptions he might make regarding her susceptibility. She thought he thought he was irresistible, and it was useless to try and

217

tell her that his work was his work, and his life was whatever, wherever he cared to make it. He was an actor, and he had come into contact, in the course of his career, with scores of beautiful women; they had been co-stars, colleagues; sometimes they had been more—but he was aware that he had never before, outside his professional orbit, met a woman who had disturbed or distracted him for more than a moment.

Until now.

He could tell her that, and she would regard it merely as another dip into his actor's box of tricks. If he said that she was beautiful, desirable, if he told her that he loved her, that he wanted to marry her, that he wanted to go upstairs and pull that pale imitation of a man out of his bed and throw him out of the window, she would think that he was piqued at her aloofness and anxious to break down her barriers. There was nothing he could say that she would believe; the more convincing it sounded, the more she would applaud the act.

He moved aside and opened the door for her.

"Good night," he said. "I'll be leaving Wood Mount in the morning, but I would like to thank you for—"

"We have to thank you," she broke in abruptly, and then without another word, walked past him and out of the room.

He closed the door behind her, kicked two chairs savagely into place and stood staring down at the table.

He would be leaving Wood Mount—but he wouldn't be going far. He was going as far as the George Inn at Greenhurst—and, for the moment, no further. This thing wasn't finished yet. He had no wish to entangle himself with the man up there whose measurements were, to his mind, so short of those he regarded as requisite in a partner for Lucille. But he had got into this thing and he had got in deeper than he knew... until to-night. Driving back after leaving her here with another man, driving back alone, with the faint scent of her still in the car, the warmth and excitement of her still stirring his senses, he had known exactly how much, how deeply, he had come to be involved.

This thing was not finished; not by a long way. It was a race, now—and there could be no dead-heat in the marriage stakes. There could be only one winner. Only one nose could get past the post.

And, God helping him, it was not going to be the Digby nose.

Chapter Fifteen

Breakfast was not a comfortable meal, but Lucille, looking at the assorted elements seated round the table, felt that things might have been a good deal worse. She and Digby were the first down; the others came in one by one and Digby, she was forced to acknowledge, tried his best with each. The fact that he had made little impression on them discouraged her, but she was not greatly surprised. If she herself, in the last few hours, had begun to feel that the members of her family had formed themselves into a complete unit with herself on the outside, how could Digby, a stranger and a newcomer, hope to fix their attention on himself? Roselle sat dreaming of Jeff; Simon was engrossed in Long John, Dominic intent upon his food. Julia considered that she had done enough by entertaining Digby for a crushingly boring half-hour the night before; it was now somebody else's turn. Nicholas...he was not impressed, Lucille could see.

But if Digby did not excite admiration, she could feel thankful at least that his was not a personality to rouse the children's antagonism. They greeted him, answered his enquiries as to their health with detached politeness, and forgot him.

Robert Debrett was by far the most comfortable among the grown-ups at the table. He went to the kitchen to superintend Pietro's cooking of his omelette, and bore it to his place to eat it. He gave Digby a brief summary of the beauty spots in the neighbourhood—none of which he himself had seen—and regretted that he could not stay and drive him round. This was the first indication the others had had of his imminent departure, and Lucille saw that Digby missed nothing of their blank dismay at the prospect. Robert let the clamour go on for some time before he stilled it with the assurance that he was going to remove himself only as far as the George at Greenhurst.

"Good-oh, good-oh," said Dominic. "Lucille, can't I have an omelette like Robert's got?"

"No. Julia," said Lucille, "there's cereal—don't you want it?"

"I'll go back to it," said Julia.

"You'll start with it," said Nicholas.

"Oh, all *right*. Lucille, Pietro says I can be his assistant in the kitchen and learn all about Italian food; can I?"

"If Pietro doesn't mind, why should I?"

"You won't make a proper cook; you're too messy," Dominic informed his sister. "Here, Long John. Look, he *likes* corn flakes!"

"You're not to feed him at the table," said Simon angrily. "Stop it, Dominic!"

"I'm not feeding him! All I gave him was one teeny, wee-

221

ny corn flake, that's all. Look—he wants more."

"Well, he can't have it," said Simon. "He isn't to beg."

"He isn't *begging*," denied Dominic. "He's just *asking*."

"You're *not* to *feed* him," repeated Simon. "He never used to beg at meals, and..." His words were suddenly addressed to the dog. "No, Long John! No. *Trust!*"

The morsel was a mere two inches away from Long John's round, black nose. The word stabbed through his keen anticipation and, incredulous, he looked up at his master through the curtain of shagginess.

"No. Trust!" repeated Simon.

Long John sank slowly down and remained flattened on the floor, his eyes almost crossed in his yearning contemplation of the tit-bit so near to them. A long, sad sigh escaped him—a shudder of resignation. There it was—a mere tongue's-length away. But he couldn't have it. That was life for you. Dog's life.

"You're cruel," said Julia, indignantly to Simon.

"No, I'm not. Long John knows it's wrong to go snuffling at people at table. He never used to do it."

"Well, I'll take him out after breakfast and play ball with him," promised Julia. "I will, Long John darling— I will. Ball, fellow!"

"You're coming out with me," Nicholas told her, leaning across to hand his cup to Lucille for refilling.

"Where to?" asked Julia in surprise.

"We're going to see the Headmistress of the school in

Greenhurst. Uncle Bill fixed an appointment for us," said Nicholas.

It was some time before Julia could speak at all, so unexpected, so crushing was the blow. Mouth open, fork dropping with a clatter onto her plate, she gazed at her brother, speechless.

"A *school*?" she gasped, finally. "A *school*?"

"Did you think you'd finished with them?" asked Nicholas.

"But...but..." Julia's mind darted in search of life-lines. "But I haven't got any proper clothes to put on! Only my other school clothes, and you can't go to other schools in other school clothes!"

"You can take off the distinguishing marks," said Nicholas. "We leave the house at eleven."

"But—" A ray of hope illuminated Julia's countenance. "They won't have me," she stated with confidence. "I've only just been expelled."

"But you didn't do anything bad." said Dominic in an attempt at reassurance that drew upon him the full glare of Julia's wrath.

"I didn't ask *you* to say anything," she shouted. "Why don't you mind your own beastly business?"

"Quiet," said Nicholas. "And finish your breakfast. You'll need your strength."

"You can't just go into a school just like that," said Julia, pushing food down agitatedly. "You have to take an entrance exam, and I'll fail—I know I'll fail. I'll—Oh, Lucille..." she wailed, "why should I have to go to another school straight away?"

"It's awfully nice, Julia," said Roselle. "You'll like it."

"No, I shan't," said Julia morosely. "You may have liked school, but I never did—and they won't like me, either. I bet they'll hate me—School!" The word was a desolate cry. "School! Bells, bells, stinking bells! Chapel and games, and no time to yourself. Gruesome uniform and beastly bossy mistresses!"

"And lessons," said Nicholas. "Don't leave out those."

"Oh, Lucille—couldn't I stay at home and have a governess, like girls used to in the olden days? Couldn't I, Lucille."

"No," said Nicholas. "Cheer up—Lucille and Roselle survived their schooldays, and there's no reason why you shouldn't."

"But some girls"—Julia leaned across the table to emphasise the point—"some girls *like* school, Nicholas, honestly they do! But other girls...girls like me, don't get on at all well in them. If you'll tell me what lessons to do, I'll do them, truly I will. I'll work like mad."

"That's the spirit," said Nicholas. "Let's get to the school with those words still echoing. And now get a move on."

"I—I don't feel very well," said Julia. "I've got an awful pain suddenly."

"That's tough," said Nicholas. "You must go and lie down—when we get back."

Hope died, and Julia sat hunched in despair. The others were silent; Simon looked across at Lucille thoughtfully for some moments and then made a wary circle round the point on which he wanted enlightenment.

"Lucille—"

"Yes, Simon!"

"I was only wondering," said Simon, "about me and Dominic. I mean, will we have to go to new schools, like Julia?"

It was Nicholas who answered the question.

"You'll go—eventually—to my old school," he said. "But there's no hope of getting you in straight away like Julia. She's the lucky one; you and Dominic will have to wait until the school's ready to take you—to wit, next term."

"Is Julia's a day school?" said Dominic.

"Yes."

"But how will she get there?" asked Simon.

"She'll get there on a bicycle."

"Yes—but where from?"

There was a moment's pause, and then Nicholas spoke quietly.

"From here," he said.

There was complete silence in the room. Julia, her mind swept clean of her own affairs, could only stare. Simon had turned white; Dominic had a good deal to say, but was having difficulty in deciding where to begin. Lucille, watching them, saw that as the full import of Nicholas's words went home to them, they turned and looked at the person they recognised, by guess or by intuition, to be the one most affected by the news—herself. But she saw, with a pang, that there was no surprise in their expressions. There was curiosity, there was relief—but it was, in their opinion, the obvious solution, one to be taken almost for granted. Something nice had happened, they seemed to say; the house won't be sold, but we knew all the time that it wouldn't...

Julia was the first to speak.

"When will you get married and go away?" she asked Lucille in simple curiosity.

"Soon, I suppose," smiled Digby, putting down the cup of coffee which, with a piece of toast, was all he took at breakfast.

"Will you like it there?" enquired Dominic of Lucille.

"We hope so," smiled Digby again. "And I hope you'll remember that then you'll have two homes instead of one."

It was gracefully said, but Lucille was feeling the effect of a double shock; she had known nothing of the arrangement made by Nicholas to see the school; he must have learned of the appointment after she had left the Milwards last night. And this sudden, this completely public announcement of it was made, she knew, to cut the ground from under her feet—to prevent arguments, to bring her face to face with the fact that there was, in fact, to be no argument; she had made her plans for the future, and Nicholas had made his.

She saw, dimly, that he had acted with promptness and good sense. Her fiancé and her fiancés's mother were unknown quantities, and however helpful they might turn out to be, they could not provide a home for the children. It was not Lucille's own house—it was old Mrs. Russell's, and the children could be no more than welcome visitors. Their own home was here; she wondered miserably how she could ever have thought otherwise. They had no home but this—and now she was leaving it, but Nicholas had stepped into her place, and they were all going to stay here with him.

She felt sick and shaken, but hardest of all to bear was the relief she had heard in Digby's voice after Nicholas had made his announcement. After one meal with them, after less than an hour in their company, he showed plainly that the noise and confusion, the caper-and-toss of a healthy and boisterous family, was not his idea of gracious living. He had done his best: the dog had snuffled on the knife-crease of his trousers and he had said nothing; Julia had flicked shreds of corn-flakes on to his sleeve and he had quietly removed them. He had made several attempts to interest the children in intelligent subjects, and each attempt had fallen thuddingly flat. He had done his best to seem amused by Pietro's dramatic entrances from the kitchen with refills for the hot dishes; he had asked Roselle for the milk and the sugar, and had made no complaint when she had passed him the salt and marmalade instead. Everything that patience and amiability could do, he had done—but if this chaos was to be repeated at every meal, his aloof countenance said plainly, he would prefer a tray in the study.

Lucille struggled to be just: he was an only child, she reminded herself, and he lived in a morgue. She had looked forward to opening the closed windows of his house, his life, and letting in stimulating draughts of fresh air; he was kind, but he was not gay because he had never had gay companionship. His evenings were passed with his mother and the Third Programme, and it was not his fault that he had more than a touch of heaviness. She—she and the children—could have made him smile, made him younger...

She and the children. But the children, she knew now, would not come—or if they came once, they would not return. She had no home to offer them, and she could not—at this late stage—go back on her assurances to Digby that she would not mind living with his mother in his mother's house. She had not liked the thought at first, but he had convinced her of its soundness—she had been bound to admit that it was simple, sensible, economical.

She had thought, without knowing that she thought it, that the arrangement would not be for long; Mrs. Russell was old, and old ladies did not last for ever. But now, in a flash of blinding certainty, Lucille knew that some old ladies did—and that Mrs. Russell would. She would go on, tough, indestructible, until Lucille's youth was over, until Digby had settled immovably into dullness and middle-age.

The family—here at Wood Mount.

Herself—with the Russells down in Cornwall....

She lifted her head to find Robert Debrett's eyes on her, studying her quietly, and into her answering glance she tried to put all the anger and despair and frustration that filled her, all her dim conviction that this was, in some way, his fault.

Her reason told her that he had nothing to do with it— her instinct told her that his presence among them at this crucial time had been responsible for the confidence, the ease and assurance with which Nicholas had arranged their future. The ideas had come from Nicholas, but if Robert Debrett had not been here to back him, encourage him, Nicholas would not have found sufficient courage to act so effectively. She would have put forward alternative schemes, Mr. Milward would have urged caution, Jeff would have bided his time. It was Robert Debrett—cool, poised, completely sure of himself—who had provided the stiffening. He might not have said much—he might not have said anything—but he had shown Nicholas clearly that he thought his course was the right one.

Perhaps she ought to be grateful. Perhaps this was just what they had all needed: a man of wide knowledge and experience, sufficiently interested in them to want to help—to guide. Perhaps, if she could see clearly, she would see that this role was the one that Digby might have, should have filled. Perhaps it was her own fault that Digby had proved so totally inadequate—perhaps her own decisiveness had led him to believe that no guidance and no help was needed.

But the fact remained; Digby was sitting here beside her at the table, looking like a man whose troubles were at an end.

He was relieved—he was deeply thankful to know that Simon and Julia and Dominic...and Long John...would not shatter for long the peace of his home. It was too late for him to adapt himself to a large and growing family; he had been reared to quietness and good behaviour, and no doubt he felt at this moment as though he had just breakfasted in the jungle—or at the Zoo.

Robert Debrett's eyes were still on her, and she became aware, to her horror, that there was no anger and no reproach in her glance: there was only a desperate appeal. She had no clear idea of what she was asking him—or telling him; she knew only that the panic in her heart had shown for a moment in her eyes as she looked at him.

She came out of a trance to realise that the others had gone out, leaving her with Digby in the dining room. He was watching her, and seemed about to say something, but Lucille could hear Jeff's voice, and she knew that Nicholas had met him in the hall and had taken him into the drawing-room, and that Robert and Roselle were in there too.

An overwhelming sense of her isolation swept over her. It was too sudden, this severance, she thought desolately. They had all accepted the fact of her marriage without either congratulation or regret; they were behaving as though it had taken place, as though she were already gone.

She got up and walked across the hall and went into the drawing-room, and Digby, after some hesitation, followed her. Lucille made no attempt to approach the subject by a circuitous route: she faced Nicholas and released something of her feeling of reproach.

"You've worked fast," she told him.

He looked at her.

"Yes," he admitted. "But—"

"And without a word to me."

"I told you exactly what I was going to do," he said "The only surprise is that I did it."

"You had no right to do anything definite without talking it over with me."

"I've got your letter in my pocket," he said mildly. "You'd given orders for the sale of Wood Mount before you had so much as asked us all what we thought of the idea. You meant well, but you forgot that even if you didn't want to live here any more we might want to."

"I told you that we couldn't...that I thought we couldn't afford to keep the house. If you had any other ideas, I was the person you ought to have discussed them with."

"Why, Lucille? You've done your whack for us all, and I'm damn grateful and I think you did a good job. Now it's up to me to let you get out with a clear mind— a clear conscience, if you like. It was nice of Digby here to offer to take us all in, but it wouldn't have worked. Now you can be at ease; be happy; we can look in on you and you can look in on us and you'll be able to feel that everything's ironed out nicely. I'm only sorry you dragged Digby all this way for nothing."

"Not for nothing," said Digby politely. "I wanted to meet you all, rather."

Lucille stared at her brother. She wanted to ask him where he was getting money from; he could not take over a house and a family, pay household bills, pay school bills without money. If she asked him...if he said that Robert Debrett...a wave of fury rose and almost choked her...then she would forget her upbringing and she would personally throw every penny back in Robert's handsome, calm, unreadable countenance.

She heard Jeff clearing his throat nervously and turned to face him.

"I came to tell you, Lucille," he said, "that...well, as a matter of fact, the house...the house has been sold." Bewilderment, shock, a feeling of utter misery swung the drawing-room round Lucille and settled it again at a somewhat crooked angle.

"Sold?" she managed to ask.

"Last night," said Nicholas.

She stared at him, comprehension beginning to creep into her mind.

"Who...bought it?" she asked.

"I did," said Robert.

"I did," said Jeff.

"I did," said Nicholas. "We all did. All three of us. We put down one-third of the price apiece—roughly. In case you're wondering where my share came from, I'll tell you: from the

Bank. A little thing called a mortgage. The house fetched eight thousand: three thousand from Robert, three from Jeff, the other two from me. The Bank got a bit stuffy about security, and Uncle Bill said he'd take care of that. I'm keeping a third of the house for myself and the three kids; Jeff and Roselle are having their bit, and Robert's putting a bathroom in the top flat and using it as a week-end and holiday home for the sole purpose of keeping in touch with Pietro's cooking. Pietro's a fixture, and so is Corny—Miss Cornhill. She ought to go, she says, but she can't make herself do it. And so there you are. You can have a lovely wedding—and none of us hanging round your neck."

He stopped, and nobody spoke for some minutes. Lucille could not have spoken if she had tried; the others were silent, watching her.

At last, clearing his throat a little importantly, Digby decided to voice the appreciation of the Russells.

"I'd like to say," he began, and found the words dying on his lips. Lucille was looking at him, and the expression on her face was so...he groped, rejected and finally settled for ferocious. She did, he thought in astonishment; she looked positively ferocious.

"Please keep out of this," she said in a low, dangerous voice. "This is nothing whatsoever to do with you. It's between Nicholas and myself and nobody—*nobody* else."

"Except Jeff and Roselle and Robert," Nicholas reminded her.

The hot, tight feeling in Lucille's throat moved to a spot behind her eyes. She felt them smarting, and knew with a sort of horror that in a moment she was going to open her mouth and cry. No, not cry; howl, she told herself in panic. She was going to open her mouth and howl like a dog, howl because it was all over and settled; finished, tied up to everybody's satisfaction—except her own. She was free; she could marry Digby and live happily with him and his mother and Bach and Beethoven and all the other great masters. Her way was clear.

And she was going to howl like a dog.

But not here. Not in front of them all. Not with Robert Debrett's cool, quiet, all-seeing eyes upon her. Not with this feeling in her mind that he had done this— somehow—to force her hand. She was too confused to think, too miserable to speak, too panic-stricken to stay with them all looking at her.

She turned and walked past them to the door. Robert opened it for her and she passed him without a word.

He closed the door. Digby walked to a window and stood gazing out abstractedly, his thoughts far from pleasant. His mother had often hinted...but this display of...really, she had looked almost frighteningly fierce. Nobody could apply the term virago to the woman one was about to marry; nobody would dream of referring to her youngest brothers and sister as savages, but really! Perhaps his mother had been...

He was aware that Nicholas was speaking to him, and turned.

"I'm sorry we've inflicted so much of this family problem on you," he was saying.

Digby looked at him and managed a weak—a very weak smile.

"No, no...not at all," he said.

"Lucille often goes off with a bang," said Nicholas, "but it doesn't last long. You mustn't take any notice."

"No—ah, no. Of course not," said Digby. "But—"

"So don't let it worry you."

"No, no. It's just...it's just—it's just that one's upset, rather," Digby confided.

Chapter Sixteen

Digby had allowed himself four days at Wood Mount; two were to be devoted to clearing up any unfinished business there might be over the unlooked-for return of Lucille's brothers and sisters; the other two he planned to give to the agreeable task of getting better acquainted with his future sisters and brothers-in-law.

He saw with relief on his arrival that Nicholas had relieved him of the first duty; he therefore applied himself to the second with zeal and goodwill, but went to bed every night with the feeling that as far as getting to know the family was concerned, he was no further on than if he had stayed at home in Cornwall—and he was beginning to wish very much that he had done so.

He had chosen Nicholas for the first of his friendly overtures; he found him pleasant but, he thought, somewhat frivolous; conversations with him seemed to run in aimless circles. He had enquired about the possibilities of a job, and Nicholas had smiled happily.

"One'll turn up," he said.

"Yes," said Digby, "of course. But had you any particular leads in mind?"

"Leads?"

"Shall we say ideas, plans, hopes?"

They were in the garden and they were both seated in the same kind of deck chair, but Digby was sitting upright in his, while Nicholas had lowered his almost to the ground, and was lying, rather than sitting in it, basking in the warm sunshine.

"Hopes?" he repeated. "Oh, yes, plenty of those."

"Is there anyone to whom you can apply—anyone who has influence anywhere?"

"Not a soul," said Nicholas cheerfully. "We're not awfully well set up with influential contacts. Lovely things, dragonflies, aren't they?"

"Beautiful. Has Mr. Milward suggested anything?"

"Uncle Bill? Well, if the worst comes to the worst, he'll give me a desk in his outer office and let me interview clients."

"Finding the right job is a fairly serious matter."

"It is. Thank the Lord I've got my trumpet. I can always stand outside a pub and send Julia round with the hat. It would have to be Julia, because she's the only one who could make them fork out. I might have a shot outside the George. Incidentally, you're coming to dinner there with us on Tuesday evening, aren't you?"

"Mr. Debrett was kind enough to invite me, yes."

"He's giving a return show to Uncle Bill and Aunt Maggie. Lucille wanted to have it here, but Robert said No; it was to be his party at the George. When do you go back?"

"I shall have to leave on Wednesday, I'm afraid. May I take this opportunity of saying how glad I am that things have turned out so well as regards the house? Lucille and I will be very happy if things go well here."

"Not as happy as I'll be," commented Nicholas. "But it was a damn silly idea to sell, anyway. Lucille has them, sometimes."

"She was acting for the best."

"She thought she was. I wish she was getting married from here. A girl ought to be married from her own home."

"It was a long way to bring my mother; she isn't strong, you know."

"Then it's a good thing Lucille didn't install me and my trumpet in her house, don't you think? Or is she a jazz fiend?"

"I don't think," said Digby carefully, "that one could call her a jazz fiend."

"Then she's had a lucky escape. Especially as Julia's turned musical too."

Digby gave a slight shudder. Julia had without warning decided to develop a latent talent for music; she sat at the piano in the drawing room hour after hour, groping for the notes of a piece called the March, March, March of the Mulligan Guards—learned, she said, from an ancient gardener at the Convent. With the Mulligan Guards in the drawing room and

Sweet Adeline up in Nicholas's bedroom, Digby felt that the time could not go too quickly for him and bring the day of his return to a quieter and more congenial atmosphere.

He sat silent, seeing for the first time the appalling consequences that might have followed his rash promise to Lucille. He had assured her, in all good faith, that his home would be open to her brothers and sisters during their holiday periods. His home was large, and he was prepared to extend them a welcome. But the invitation had been tendered, he now realised, because he had had no idea what kind of brothers and sisters they were. Now he knew. It was a wonder that he had survived the visit at all, and a greater wonder that his sanity was unimpaired. Meals had been torture, with that Italian buffoon prancing in and out with unsuitable food; his attempts to become acquainted with Lucille's family had met with inattention and yawns.

He tried to assess the situation fairly; his own upbringing, he realised, had been an exceptionally gentle one. There had been nothing in his life—nothing, indeed, in his experience—of the noisy, the tempestuous conditions that existed at Wood Mount. His mornings at home were decorous—he almost said decent; he rose, took his bath and went downstairs to breakfast, all in a peaceful and orderly-manner. He had never before wakened to the sound of angry thumps on the bathroom doors, with the yells of those who wished to enter drowned by the protests of those who were not yet ready to come out. He had no idea that civilised children engaged in scuffles on the landing in the morning, or pillow fights in their bedrooms at night. On his first morning at Wood Mount, Julia had brought him his morning tea; it was a kindness he had asked her not to repeat. She had begun by kicking his door vigorously.

"Digby! Dig-by! I've got a tray with things on it, and I can't open the door."

"Oh, you fathead—I'll do it." That was Dominic. "There you are."

"All right; now you can shut it again or people'll see him in bed." That was Julia, entering. "Good morning, Digby; Lucille sent me up with your tea in case you wanted it."

"Er—thank you, Julia."

"Aren't you going to sit up? Then I can put the tray on top of you."

"Well...just put it on the table for now."

"But then you won't be able to reach it!"

"I'll get up later."

"What's the use of getting up if you're supposed to have tea in bed?" asked Julia reasonably. "Sit up and then you can take it."

He sat up; if she didn't feel embarrassed at seeing a stranger in his night attire, there was perhaps no reason for his own strong dislike of exposing it.

"Here you are. Tea and fruit. Lucille says what else?"

"Nothing, thank you. This is—this is splendid."

"The papers haven't come because they weren't ordered

240

because of the house being shut up. Do you want the bathroom first or not, Nicholas says. There's another one, but Robert's in it."

"When everybody has finished..."

"Gosh! you'd better go in before Dominic—he leaves the bath simply gruesome. Shall I draw your curtains?"

"No thank you."

"I think I'd better; then the lovely sun'll come in. There. You're not as hairy as Nicholas, are you?

"Er..."

"If you want anything, thump on the floor. Oh, Pietro wanted to bring up your tea, but Lucille wouldn't let him because he hasn't got a razor to shave with yet and he looks awfully wild. Thump, will you?"

"Thank you, Julia."

Simon was gentler than this, but getting to know Simon, Digby discovered, involved getting to know his dog. Dogs were dogs, and there were one or two breeds that fitted charmingly into the domestic scene—even into a drawing-room—but this enormous, shaggy animal of unknown parentage and embarrassingly friendly disposition...it was quite, quite out of the question. Dominic—he was a nice little boy, but his one interest in life seemed to be located a hundred feet above the ground. A fine piece of work, the tree house, no doubt—but to climb up in these clothes...no.

Roselle? She was never at home; the young man, Jeff,

came to fetch her each morning and bore her off into Green-hurst. Lucille...

Yes, Lucille. Lucille, he was certain, was avoiding him.

There was no doubt, Digby acknowledged to himself, that she was behaving very oddly. Matters had been settled to everybody's satisfaction, and the future was clear—but she seemed to be under more strain now than she had been when the problem was still unsolved. It was natural that she should feel uneasy at leaving them before Nicholas had got a job—but until he was left alone with his new responsibilities, it was not likely that he would realise their seriousness. While Lucille was here to direct the household, he would go on playing his trumpet. If she would take his advice and come back to Cornwall as soon as possible the family would settle down under the new conditions.

But Lucille refused—unaccountably—to discuss the matter; worse, he had scarcely had a word with her since his arrival.

Tuesday came, and they had had no time whatsoever to themselves; on the morrow he was to go home.

Home. He felt all the longing, all the keen anticipation that Nicholas had felt on approaching Wood Mount three days earlier. He had all the aching desire that Roselle had felt to leave uncongenial surroundings and return to familiar things. He was ready to muster as much courage as Julia should anything arise to prevent his leaving here.

But nothing, he knew, would prevent his leaving. The

Waynes, he saw with sudden clarity, would see him go with the same total lack of interest they had shown in his arrival. His journey had been made for nothing; for worse than nothing—for if he had stayed at home, he would not now have been weighed down with these feelings of uneasiness and apprehension.

He faced the fact with curiosity as his chief emotion, and went on to speculate about Robert Debrett. A woman might lose her head for a time over a man like that; he was a handsome fellow, and he knew how to play on people's susceptibilities. But he had been in the house only twenty-four hours before his own arrival, and to do him justice, he seemed to spend as much time with the others as with Lucille. He had said nothing about leaving Greenhurst—that might be a point to look into. But enquiries might lead to the suspicion that he was jealous—and he was not; not in the least....

At this point, Digby felt it unsafe to examine his feelings too closely. He knew only that he was not happy—but he was in alien surroundings and an alien atmosphere, and he would no doubt recover his serenity the moment he reached home. And although people might call his home too quiet and his life almost dull, he himself, after this brief but revealing glimpse of what family life could be, was only too ready to return to dullness. Perhaps, ten or fifteen years ago...No. Not even then. This kind of life was not for him. He needed peace; he liked long, quiet hours in which to read, to talk on serious and interesting matters, to listen to beautiful music. He needed the blessed feeling of being alone, or being with quiet people. He wanted to be in his dim library at home, watching his mother seated in her high-backed chair at the other side of the fire-place— slim, silent and utterly dignified. Even to imagine Nicholas and his trumpet in that setting was a horror from which he shrank—and yet he had agreed to throw his home open to them all...

It had been madness, and he could not be too grateful to the Providence that had sent Nicholas to Wood Mount in time.

He had been mad—but he had regained most of his sanity. It only remained for him to go home and discover how much madness still remained....

Digby was the only adult at Wood Mount who had any lingering doubts about the situation. Robert Debrett was quite clear on all points but one: how he was to extricate Lucille from an unsuitable engagement.

That she had appealed to him, he was completely certain. She had not meant to—but she had been frightened, and she had turned to him with an unspoken plea. He had not answered it—as yet. There was nothing to be done yet; Digby was going away, and it was only necessary to see that Lucille did not follow him. He would be here to see to that.

He thought of taking Nicholas into his confidence, but rejected the idea. Nicholas had done enough; the rest was his own affair. For the present, things weren't going too badly; Pietro and Miss Cornhill were on his side, and were proving invaluable in leading him with apparent unconsciousness to wherever Lucille happened to be, and then melting softly, magically away. Miss Cornhill had said nothing in words; Pietro had said everything, but he had said it to Robert at the George and had not presumed to repeat it at Wood Mount.

It would work out, decided Robert. She loved him; if she didn't, she wouldn't have allowed him to stay in Greenhurst. A word from her would have sent him away—but she had not said it. That was enough. She thought, the poor sweet, that she was stuck with Digby; there was nothing to be done about that at the moment. If the fellow hadn't been so likeable, one could have been ruthless— but in his pale, boneless way he was a nice chap and God knows he was doing his best to keep his head above water. There was no need to make things worse for him. Let him go home in peace; he would learn soon enough that Lucille was not for him.

They had only to wait and the thing would work itself out.

This assumption proved to be correct—but not even Robert guessed how short a time was to elapse before Fate, in the unlikely person of Mr. Joey Helyon, took a hand in the affair.

Robert had planned his dinner party as a return for the Milwards' hospitality, a table for eight—Robert, Mr. and Mrs. Milward and Jeff, Lucille, Roselle, Nicholas and Digby— waited in a quiet corner of the dining-room, and the landlord had fallen in with his wish for quietness in all respects but one: the band, which played only on Saturdays, should play to-night to mark the occasion as one of congratulation to young Mr. Milward and his future wife; they were both well known and liked by the hotel staff, and to this much, perhaps, Mr. Debrett would agree.

Robert agreed, and drove out to Wood Mount to drive his guests into Greenhurst. They could all have fitted with ease into his car, but Nicholas chose to use his newly-mended motor bike and side-car and Digby, on an impulse which he could not quite analyse, and which seemed to spring from a sudden reluctance to make use of Robert Debrett's sumptuous limousine, elected to go in the side car.

Robert and his passengers drove off; Nicholas was still in his room, giving a last twist to his bow tie; Digby waited for him in the drawing room.

Robert shepherded Lucille and Roselle into the large, low-ceilinged lounge of the George, and they were joined by the Milwards. They sat round in a circle, almost the only party there, but presently there was heard the arrival of a large and noisy group of people, and soon they saw them enter the lounge—eight men, led by their large, cheerful, loud-voiced host.

Robert glanced at the man and their eyes met. The next moment Joey had detached himself from his friends and was crossing the room with outstretched hand and a delighted shout.

"Well, well, well, chase me round the block, if it isn't Robert himself!" He reached Robert, seized his hand and gave him a thump on the shoulder. "Robert my boy, my long-lost boy, what in the name of turtle soup are you doing here?"

Robert smiled, and noted with some relief that Joey and his friends were sober; Joey's exuberance was due to his being in an especially expansive mood, and extremely pleased with life.

"I'm staying here," he told him. "Now go away, Joey; I'll talk to you afterwards."

"What—no introduction to your friends, Robert boy?" Joey looked round the circle wistfully. "A blonde, a redhead, and no introductions? Oh, don't be greedy Robert," he protested. "My friends are your friends and you ought to tell them who I am. I'll tell them. I'm the boy," he informed them all, "who put this fellow Debrett on the map. I made him famous. I was the cameraman who was on the job when he made his first big success; I was the boy who shot the scenes that shot him to stardom. Me, Joey H." He turned towards his party. "Here, boys! Here, boys! Come and meet Robert and his friends."

"No, Joey." Robert spoke appealingly. "This is a nice private little celebration."

"Celebration? Celebrating what, Robert boy?"

"An engagement. We've got—"

"An engagement! Ho, ho, ho!" roared Joey in delight. "You sly puss, you! Now which is the bride—the blonde or the red-head? Is it the blonde you've captured, Robert my son?"

"No, Joey. For Pete's sake will you—"

"Then it's the red-head!" roared Joey. "Robert, she's beautiful, she's beautiful, she's beautiful!" He was round at Lucille's side, his voice dropping to a gentle murmur, his round, red face beaming with fatherly delight. "Robert's darling, will you tell me your name?"

"My name's Lucille, but—"

"Lucille." Joey caressed the sound—then he turned away and his voice rose to a joyous bellow. "Boys! Come on, gather round, gather round. We're going to drink to Robert and Lucille! Where's the waiter? Charlie, champagne! Where's the band? Charlie, get 'em out here, will you? Get 'em out here and let's hear 'em. Come on now, fellers, get round, get round."

Robert eyed his guests. The Milwards were smiling; few people could resist Joey's warm-hearted manner; he was noisy, but he was patently sincere; he might have other friends in other places, but for the moment they were forgotten; his old friend Robert Debrett was here, and in the happiest circumstances.

Robert was aware that he could check Joey with a word— the right word. But he was thinking fast, and it seemed to him that this misunderstanding was leading them all towards some kind of climax, perhaps towards some clearer understanding of their problems. He would, he decided, let it go on.

He looked at Lucille; Joey had drawn her gently but irresistibly to her feet, and was leading her into the centre of his group of friends; now he was coming back for Robert, and soon the two had been placed side by side, drink in hand, while round them were gathered a host of well-wishers, enthusiastically toasting them.

Robert gave a slight shrug; it indicated, as he meant it to indicate, that he felt it wiser, for the moment, to let Joey have his head. This would soon be over, he seemed to say; it was one of those misunderstandings that it was less trouble to accept than to argue about. He looked down at Lucille, and smiled.

"If you can bear this," he said, under cover of Joey's speech, "then I can."

She said nothing; her eyes were on the hotel entrance, and Robert, following her glance, saw that Nicholas and Digby had come in and were standing watching the scene.

"And so," roared Joey in conclusion, "I ask you to drink to the happy couple. Robert and Lucille. Robert and his lovely red-head. Long life and happiness!"

"Long life and happiness," echoed the company.

"And now you may kiss her, Robert boy," said Joey. "But me first."

He placed a soft, paternal kiss on Lucille's cheek, and then turned her towards Robert.

"She's yours, my boy," he pronounced." "Kiss her— kiss her, can't you?"

Robert looked over the heads of the company and met Digby's glance briefly; then he bent and laid his lips on Lucille's. Then, handing his glass and hers to Joey, he took her in his arms and did the thing more thoroughly.

At the door, Nicholas turned and studied his companion curiously.

"You needn't mind," he told him. "I met this Joey fellow on my way down to Wood Mount the other day. He's got the wrong end of the stick, obviously, but Robert's quite right to let it ride—stopping Joey would be like arguing with Niagara."

Digby was not looking at Joey; his eyes, quiet, speculative, were on Robert Debrett.

"He could have stopped it...if he'd wanted to," he said.

Sharp chap, reflected Nicholas. Good brain; one had to hand it to him. In many ways one couldn't help liking him; it wasn't his fault that he'd been harnessed all his life to a neat little turn-out, and never once been allowed to get out of a trot. He would make a decent sort of husband for the right girl, but he, Nicholas, had never really thought that Lucille was the right girl.

He heard Digby's voice once more.

"Debrett," he said slowly, "seems to be making the most of it."

Robert had detached Lucille from the crowd, and was walking with her towards the two standing in the doorway. Nicholas waited for them, and led them out on to the quiet porch, shutting out the sounds of the band and the almost professional men's voice choir, now being conducted by Joey.

Outside, Nicholas was the first to speak.

"I've explained to Digby," he said, "that it was all a misunderstanding."

"And my own opinion," said Digby, "was that it could have been stopped at once if"—he looked at Robert—"if you'd wanted to stop it. Am I right?"

"Quite right," said Robert quietly.

Lucille turned to look at him.

"Then why didn't you?" she asked.

"It seemed a good chance," said Robert, "to explain what I felt about you."

"You were waiting for me to go away, I presume," said Digby, "before making it even clearer?"

"Quite right," said Robert once more.

"Aren't you talking a bit too much?" Nicholas asked him.

"I don't think so," said Robert. "It's not easy to tell a girl you love her when her fiancé's around. My idea was to let him go away and then find out whether there was any chance of making Lucille change her mind and stay here."

"An honest man might have considered coming to me first," pointed out Digby.

"I thought of it," said Robert, "but I happened to like you, and I also—since we're being honest now—had an idea that you're finding the set-up rather more than you bargained for."

"I was prepared to do my best," said Digby. "I'm not a family man and I don't pretend to be. I'll be as honest as yourself and admit that—for my mother's sake—I am relieved that

251

Wood Mount is not to be sold."

"And I'll admit that I think there's been a great deal too much of your mother's feelings about the whole thing," said Robert. "If marrying Lucille meant moving your mother to the Dower house, and installing all your in-laws, from Nicholas downwards, for Lucille's peace of mind, then you should have done it and been happy to."

"I am sorry; I cannot agree with that," said Digby.

"If somebody's got a coin," murmured Nicholas, "this could be settled in no time." He looked at his sister. "This might be something to do with you," he suggested. "Can't you say something?"

"I've got nothing to say," said Lucille, "except that if Digby doesn't like my family, he's only got to say so."

Robert took her arm and turned her gently to face him.

"Listen," he said slowly. "I love you. I would like you to know that never before—except when reading it from a script—have I asked a woman to marry me. If you love this fellow—and he's a decent chap—then say so and we'll all know where we are. But if you feel that—later on—you could get to like me, I'd be very proud to wait."

Lucille's eyes went to Digby. She put out a hand and he grasped it; with her glance resting on him, she spoke slowly and dreamily.

"I have an idea," she said, "that I'm about to be jilted."

Digby smiled at her—an uncertain but singularly sweet

smile.

"I love you very much, Lucille," he said, "but—"

"—but there are other things—yes?" she said.

"Yes."

There were other things. There was peace for the spirit, there was the peace of body and mind in which he had once lived and in which he might live again. Beauty had been within his grasp, but the price of keeping it was too high—too high for him to pay.

He raised Lucille's hand for a moment to his lips, and the gesture was oddly dignified. Then he placed it in Robert's and, turning, went down the steps of the Inn and walked towards a taxi. He would drive in it to Wood Mount; it would wait for him while he brought down his suitcase; it would take him to the station and then—thank God—he would be on his way home.

Home. Away from the tumult; back to the library with its shaded lights; back to his gracious, silver-haired, queenly mother; back to his books and his pictures and his music.

He had meant to look back as the taxi drove away, but he forgot—he was lost in contemplation of this happy future.

He was driven away, and he was utterly content.

The Blue Sky of Spring

by

Elizabeth Cadell

Cliff Hermann eased his big car round the curve of the narrow country road, came face to face with a farm cart, pulled up within a yard of it, and prayed that he might soon find himself back on the wide stretches of an American highway.

English roads, he reflected bitterly, backing into the hedge, were fine for wagons or for horse-back riding—just fine—but for speedy, modern travel, they were jokes, and not funny ones. How those old-time coaches ever got along…but no; the coaches had not used these corkscrew lanes; they had kept to the main roads. They had been travelling, moreover, to places with names that people knew: Deal, Dover, Portsmouth, Bath. They were not, like himself, on the way to a small country town that nobody had ever heard of.

He had a strong impulse to turn and go back to London. He had telephoned before lunch to say that he would come down, but he had done so only because the weather had looked too bad to permit him to carry out any of his other engagements; though they had promised infinitely more enjoyment than this one, they had been out-of-doors, and the rain had been beating down with a steadiness that gave little hope for the rest of the day. But after lunch the rain had stopped; the sun had come out—and by that time it was too late to cancel his appointment to call upon this unknown Miss Dryden-Smith, at the obscure Hampshire market town of Greenhurst, with the parcel of Mexican pottery which, in a weak moment in New York, he had agreed to bring over and deliver to her while he was in England.

Well, here he was—almost. He would find this place, Greenhurst; he would drive to the Red House, he would ask for Miss Dryden-Smith, he would hand over the parcel—which could and should have been posted—and then he would make his bow and depart.

He glanced at his watch: three-ten. He should be in Greenhurst by three-thirty; he determined to be out of it again by four. That would enable him to get back to London in time to salvage some of the entertaining projects he had been obliged to jettison.

He sketched, from his experience of English country hostesses, the pattern that his visit to the Red House would follow: Miss Dryden-Smith would say Won't you sit down and How interesting it is to meet someone all the way from America and How impossible it is, don't you know, to guess from an American's accent exactly whereabouts in America he comes from, and Would he care to see the garden, and Wouldn't he care for some tea, and Perhaps he knew that living in a house like this wasn't as pleasant as it had once been, because one couldn't get servants nowadays unless one paid them enormous wages, and—

And so on and so on.

Well, he would cut all that short—very short. He wasn't, at best, an over-friendly man; he would make quick work of this Miss Dryden-Smith's attempts to detain him.

He arrived at Greenhurst just before half-past three and recalled the directions he had been given: drive straight through Main Street—they called it High Street—take the left fork and look for a big, ugly red house standing a little way back from the road.

He got to the house and rang the bell. A deaf old man admitted him, led him through a large hall to the drawing room, and ushered him into Miss Dryden-Smith's presence—and here Cliff's determination to resist hospitable pressure was checked by the realization that his hostess was not going to exert any. She was about as pleased to have him here, he saw at once, as he had been to come.

He looked at her tall, angular form and long face and decided that her expression was a degree less cordial than his own. Her manner was abrupt, her sentences brief and to the point. If he was irritated at having wasted the afternoon bringing down a valueless parcel of pottery, Miss Dryden-Smith was no less annoyed at having been compelled to remain at home in order to receive it.

"If I had known that it was going to turn out so fine," she said at once, "I would have asked you to come another day. But when you telephoned, it was raining and—"

"I'm sorry, but I couldn't have come down any other day," said Cliff. "I'm kind of busy trying to fit in a lot of business before I go back to the States. I've got quite a full programme."

He had indeed. He was booked to fly back in ten days' time, and in the meantime he hoped to fit in five cocktail parties, two dinners, three dances, a race meeting and several theatres.

"What are you doing in England?" asked Miss Dryden-Smith, without any perceptible interest in her tone.

"I'm over here to talk about a play of mine that's to be put on in London in the autumn." He stopped himself on the brink of telling her that Robert Debrett was to play the lead in it. If he mentioned Robert Debrett, her interest might be aroused—he did not think it would, but it might—and she would tell him what he already knew: that Robert Debrett had been married about a year ago in the Church whose spire was visible from these windows. Robert Debrett lived, for a great part of his time, not four miles away from Greenhurst. Robert Debrett had married Lucille Wayne, who …

He knew all that. Robert had told him. He wouldn't risk being told all over again by Miss Dryden-Smith.

"I don't know much about the theatre," she told him.

"Music, yes; drama, no."

She looked at him and took in his height and leanness, his thin, handsome face, his brooding look and his dark, almost angry looking eyes. She put his age down, accurately, as thirty-five, and wondered fleetingly whether his unapproachable manner was due to bad temper or the desire to repel too-eager advances.

"Did you drive down here?" she asked.

"Yes. Oh, you mean this?" He indicated the sling that supported one arm. "That's all right. I can use the arm quite well; I just let it rest up now and again."

"How did you hurt it?"

He told her, and as she listened, she rose and walked to the window and stood with her back to him, looking out at the wet, glistening lawn. He thought it less than polite, but he was not anxious to take up any more of her time, and said so.

"I only came down to give you the parcel—I hope the stuff in it isn't damaged," he said. "I handled it as carefully as possible."

"Thank you." She turned from the window and faced him. "Perhaps you will forgive me if I don't ask you to stay," she said. "I feel...a little tired. My heart isn't strong."

He thought, for a sardonic moment, that the words were an excuse to get rid of him—and then he saw her face, and his scepticism vanished. She looked white and drawn and, suddenly, very very old.

"If you're not feeling well," he said, "can I do anything? Call anybody?"

"No, thank you. I shall be all right. But…you must forgive me."

"Of course."

He bowed and went out, not without uneasiness, to his car. She had looked…sick. He stood uncertainly, wondering whether he ought to find the old man who had admitted him—and then he saw a middle-aged woman going in through a side gate, and watched her as she walked up to a door, opened it with the familiarity of long usage and went inside.

He got into his car and drove away. Someone was there to look after the old lady; there was no need for him to wait.

The visit had been even shorter than he had intended to make it, and as he drove down the narrow, busy little High Street, he debated whether he should go straight back to London or whether he would keep a half-promise he had made to Robert Debrett when they had met in New York. Cliff had mentioned, casually, his errand in Greenhurst—and the name of the place had brought from the usually reticent Robert Debrett a flood of information and reminiscence regarding the family into which he had married, and whose home, Wood Mount, was a few miles from the town.

On a sudden impulse, Cliff took the turning that led him past the station and along the road which Robert had told him would lead to Wood Mount. A drive of some four miles brought him to the slope on which the house stood; he saw the gate, but the building itself was hidden and it was not until he had driven past it and climbed a steep side-road that he was able to look down and see through the trees the large, beautiful white house of which he had heard so much.

He switched off the engine and sat looking down through the foliage, and into his mind came all that Robert had told him. Here lived the Waynes—all six of them—in this house in which they had been born and brought up. It was odd to think of the celebrated, sophisticated Robert Debrett in this setting—and yet Robert had come, had fallen in love with Lucille Wayne, had married her and was now mooning over her between the performances of the play in which he was acting in New York.

New York—to Greenhurst. It was a long way. Sitting in this neck of the woods, mused Cliff, sitting here with nothing to listen to but the wind and the call of the birds; with nothing moving except the branches of the trees and that little squirrel over there…yes, it was a long, long way. New York was the present and this place…this must be one of those "gleams of a remoter world" that—who was it, Shelley?—wrote about. Remote was the key-word.

Well, they could have it.

He had no intention of going to see the Waynes. The fulfilment of the half-promise he had made to Robert could, he thought, wait until his next visit to England. He was not unduly interested in country life or in family life; he had noted cautiously, as he listened to Robert, that though the three elder Waynes were reasonably adult, the other three were in or nearing their teens; he had no great wish to encounter them. Lucille, moreover, was expecting a baby; she would be in what he termed an advanced stage, and though Robert's description and proudly-displayed photographs of her proclaimed her lovely, she could not be at her best at the moment, and she would probably not be anxious to meet strangers. Next year, perhaps, he would return with a present for the baby; it would be rolling on a rug on the grass and he would bend over and tickle its bare little stomach. But for the moment…No. No Lucille. No Waynes.

He recalled other facts that he had learned from Robert. The house—this unexpectedly lovely, graceful white house—had been put up for sale about a year ago, after having been let furnished for a time. Lucille Wayne had decided to sell it—and her decision brought from afar, on the instant, unheralded, her scattered brothers and sisters, who came separately but remained to unite in a solid and unflinching front, resolved to oppose the sale. Robert had seen their arrival; Robert had stayed on to watch the subsequent struggle and in the course of it had fallen in love with the turbulent, red-haired Lucille. And now three separate units of the family lived here in their self-contained flats: up, middle and down. Cliff, his eyes on the house, tenanted each floor in turn. At the top, Lucille, and, when he returned, Robert, and, when he arrived, Robert junior. On the floor below, the sister next in age to Lucille: what was her name? Roselle. That was it; Roselle, who had married the young Greenhurst house-agent, Jeff Milward. Roselle looked like a wild rose and had all a wild rose's cooking skill. Jeff was sober and grave and wore his wild rose proudly—and got one good meal a day by lunching with his mother and father at Greenhurst.

That left the ground floor: here was where the three young ones lived, in the care of their brother Nicholas. Nicholas was...how old? He'd forgotten. Older than Roselle, who was twenty. So Nicholas was twenty plus whatever it was, and he was father and mother to the three young ones. Two boys and a girl. Julia—that was the girl. Julia stayed in the mind, somehow. Julia was the little ugly one and all the other members of the family were—so Robert said—beautiful to behold. Julia, and two boys called something and something. And there was a dog, too.

Well, there they all were. Oh—and two outsiders who had attached themselves to the family at the same time in much the same way as Robert and who now worked as cook (Italian, male) and housekeeper (English, female) on the ground floor.

And it all sounded too, too fascinating, decided Cliff, but he hadn't the time to go into it. He would leave the Waynes in their leafy retreat, and he would high-tail it back to London to some more sophisticated entertainment. Robert would understand and forgive.

He switched on the engine, backed down the narrow lane and turned the car in the direction of London. If anybody had asked him, he would have said that he was putting Greenhurst and Wood Mount and the Waynes behind him for ever.

He would have been wrong.

End of preview.

To continue reading, look for the book entitled "The Blue Sky of Spring" by Elizabeth Cadell

About the Author

Elizabeth Vandyke was born in British India at the beginning of the 20th century. She married a young Scotsman and became Elizabeth Cadell, remaining in India until the illness and death of her much-loved husband found her in England, with a son and a daughter to bring up, at the beginning of World War 2. At the end of the war she published her first book, a light-hearted depiction of the family life she loved. Humour and optimism conquered sorrow and widowhood, and the many books she wrote won her a wide public, besides enabling her to educate her children (her son joined the British Navy and became an Admiral), and allowing her to travel, which she loved. Spain, France and Portugal provide a background to many of her books, although England and India were not forgotten. She finally settled in Portugal, where her married daughter still lives, and died when well into her 80s, much missed by her 7 grandchildren, who had all benefitted from her humour, wisdom and gentle teaching. British India is now only a memory, and the quiet English village life that Elizabeth Cadell wrote about has changed a great deal, but her vivid characters, their love affairs and the tears and laughter they provoke, still attract many readers, young and not-so-young, in this twenty-first century. Reprinting these books will please her fans and it is hoped will win her new ones.

Also by Elizabeth Cadell

Made in United States
Orlando, FL
29 May 2024

47306592R00153